Cotton
ROGUE BEGINNINGS
A ROGUE ENFORCERS NOVEL

GRACE BRENNAN

COLTON

Copyright 2019 © Grace Brennan

The unauthorized reproduction or distribution of this copyrighted work is a crime punishable by law. No part of this book may be scanned, uploaded to, or downloaded from file sharing sites or distributed in any other way via the internet or any other means, electronic or print, without the publisher's permission. Criminal copyright infringement, including infringement without monetary gain, is investigated by the FBI and is punishable by up to 5 years in federal prison and a fine of $250,000.

All rights reserved. Except as permitted under the U.S. Copyright Act of 1976. No part of this publication may be reproduced, stored in, or introduced into a retrieval system or transmitted, in any form or by any means (electronic, mechanical, photocopying, recording, or otherwise), without the prior permission of Grace Brennan.

Photographer: Randy Sewell of RLS Model Images

Model: Jim Wiedenman

Cover Design & Format: Dark Water Covers

Right after I picked the name for my main character, I learned that a dear friend's son passed away—and he has the same name. I debated for a long time over whether I should change Colton's name, but with her blessing, I left it as I first envisioned it.

So this book is dedicated to Liberty Parker, and her son Colton. I never knew him, but I've heard so many amazing things, and I know the world is a dimmer place without his bright light shining around us.

Prologue

Colton Alexander clenched his jaw tightly as he stared at his cousin. Justin was sitting on the floor with his back against the wall, looking more defeated than he'd ever seen him. He searched for words, for something—anything—to say, but he kept coming up empty.

Turning away, he moved to the window, looking out at the woods behind his house. For as long as he could remember, Justin had talked about becoming an Enforcer. Enforcers were basically the shifter equivalent of human police officers, although they were more or less a mix of cop, detective, FBI agent, CIA... They were pretty much every law enforcement agency that existed all rolled into one.

They were the ones who enforced shifter laws. There weren't many laws, and pretty much all of them basically boiled down to one thing—don't terrorize others, humans especially. No hurting them, no messing with their heads, and no turning serial killer and slaughtering handfuls whenever they felt like it.

Of all their laws, that one was the most absolute, and it was one they never failed to enforce.

Not only did following the rules basically equal being a good person, since most of them were about common decency, but they were in place to protect their kind, as well. Most humans weren't aware that the supernatural, mainly shifters, even existed. They wanted to keep it that way. A shifter running around hurting their own kind and humans alike, or being too obvious about what they truly were, put the secret in jeopardy.

The last thing any of them wanted was to become the next government experiment, or to be hunted and killed because humans feared what they were.

It was a complex job that took a lot out of the lucky ones who were accepted, and it called for the best of the best. The Enforcers expected nothing less than perfection, because they wanted the odds stacked in their favor when they hunted and captured the truly evil shifters.

Becoming an Enforcer had been Justin's dream since they were kids, and he'd done his damnedest to talk Colton into it. He was so excited when it was time for them to try out, determined to give it his all and make the cut.

Only he wasn't accepted—but Colton was.

This wasn't what Colton wanted, dammit. The only reason he even tried out was because Justin asked him to. His cousin was the one who really wanted to be an Enforcer. Colton just hadn't had any idea what he wanted to do with his life yet, so he went along with it.

And now this.

It was so fucking stupid. The Enforcers should count themselves lucky that a man like Justin wanted to join them. He was hard working, determined, a hell of a fighter, and he had a heart of gold.

But his shifter gift was the ability to go without sleep if he needed to, and that wasn't good enough for them.

Picky bastards.

Every shifter had a gift, something extra that made them different from the rest. It could be physical or mental, and it could be something completely supernatural, or a human ability that was enhanced.

Colton's was the ability to manipulate the elements —earth, air, fire, and water. And it was apparently good enough for the Enforcers, because he was accepted while Justin wasn't. They were notoriously picky about choosing shifters who only had top notch gifts, but he'd never really thought they'd turn Justin down.

"You should still go to training," Justin finally said, speaking up for the first time since he'd dropped his news.

He turned to glare at his cousin. "Are you kidding? I'm not going without you."

"You should. I saw you at tryouts. You were amazing, and you passed every test with flying colors. They could use you. And the world should know that not all male dragons are dickheads. That's not something I can help with, since I got the snowy owl gene."

"I don't care if they could use me or not. I'm not helping those fuckers after they rejected you."

"Don't be a dumbass, Colt. You wouldn't be helping *them*. You'd be helping make the world a better place, for shifters and humans alike. Besides, we knew there was a chance they wouldn't accept me. We've known that since we were kids."

Shaking his head, Colton clenched his hands into fists, trying to control the anger burning inside him. "It's bullshit. They can't get anyone better than you, and to reject you because of your gift... You're more than just your gift, you know that, right?"

"Yeah, I know. But the Enforcers don't make any secret of the fact that it doesn't matter how good you are—if your gift isn't exceptional, they won't take you. It makes sense when you think about it. They have to have the odds stacked in their favor before they take on the bad guys. You and I just ignored that part of the requirements."

"I never in a million years thought they'd be stupid enough to reject you, though. I thought they'd see how much of an asset you'd be, regardless of your gift."

Justin gave him a half smile that didn't reach his blue eyes as he pushed himself to his feet. "I didn't, either; but I think we both should have seen this coming. I have to get to work, but I expect to see your bags packed when I get back. I'm serious, Colt. Go to training. Don't let me be the reason you don't become an Enforcer."

"You were the reason I even tried out to begin with, Justin. It was never my dream, and what's the point without you there?"

"Don't give me that bullshit," Justin replied, eyes narrowed. "I watched you during training, remember? It might have been my idea to get us started on this journey, but somewhere along the line my dream became yours, too. You wanted it, Colt. I could see it. And if you don't go to training, you won't get a second chance. If you decide you don't want to go through with it after that, fine. I won't say another word. But you better at least go to training before you make that decision."

Colton blew out a breath as he watched his cousin leave. Hooking his hands on his hips, he stared at the family room in the old ranch house he and Justin shared. Colton's parents were killed by dragon hunters when he was five, and he'd gone to live with his aunt and uncle. He and Justin were the same age, so they'd grown up together, more like brothers than cousins.

When Justin's parents left to move across the country, they gave the ranch to Justin and Colton. But they never imagined they'd live here long. Being ranchers in this sleepy little Montana town wasn't their destiny—becoming Enforcers and roaming the country, keeping the world safe from evil, was.

At least it had been until Justin was rejected.

And now, he didn't have a fucking clue what to do. He hated to admit it, but his cousin was right—somewhere along the line, becoming an Enforcer had turned into his dream, too. But what kind of family member—what kind of *friend*—would he be if he left Justin here alone after his dream had gotten ripped away from him forever?

What kind would you be if you left him not only hurting over losing his dream, but making him think he'd cost you yours, too? his dragon rumbled inside him. *Don't you think that'd be worse? Do what he said and go to training. Give him that much.*

Cursing, he stalked to his bedroom to pack. He was stuck between a rock and a hard place. Leaving to pursue his dream felt like intentionally hurting Justin, but his dragon was right—not going would be doing the exact same thing.

He'd do what his cousin asked, but he wasn't sure he'd be able to become a full-fledged Enforcer. As much as he wanted it, it just wouldn't feel right without Justin. And he wasn't sure he'd be able to respect anyone who could reject someone like him. They'd turned down someone who was better than anyone he'd ever met, in skills and heart, and he couldn't trust anyone with that kind of bad judgment.

This whole situation was fucked up, and he was beyond pissed that he was having to make the choices he was. As much as the Enforcers helped shifters and humans alike, as far as he was concerned, they could all go fuck themselves.

He wanted nothing to do with them.

Chapter 1

SIX YEARS LATER

Katia Evans tapped her fingers on the countertop, eyes unfocused as she gazed toward the door of the small diner where she worked. She only had one more table to clean up after the last guests paid and left before she could close and go home, and she let her mind wander as she waited. She had to; it was the only way to keep her mind off the people at the corner booth, and the way her imagination wanted to run wild at the sight of them.

She'd worked a double shift that day and her feet were sore. Normally, she wouldn't let it bother her, but it kept taking her away from the perfectly good daydream she'd been having. One where she didn't have to work two jobs to put herself through night school. Where she had a life that didn't involve seeing the diner or the old hotel she managed. One where she did more than work, go to classes, and study, snatching a few hours of sleep for herself here and there.

Grimacing, she shifted her weight, trying to take the sting away from her feet, but she knew nothing would work until she could actually sit down. Movement caught her eye and she glanced over as the men in the booth finally stood. Her eyes narrowed as one of them kept his hand on another's arm, steering him out of the door, while the third made his way to her to pay their tab.

Forcing her eyes away from the stiff set of the man's shoulders, she made herself smile at the third man, desperately trying to avoid looking into his cold brown eyes as she took his money. Whatever that was about, she didn't want to know. While this wasn't the worst part of Atlanta, it wasn't the best either, so it was always a good idea to mind her own business.

As soon as the last man paid, she rushed to the door and locked it quickly just in case, breathing a sigh of relief as she flipped the sign on the door. Walt, the cook, was in the back cleaning up so she wasn't alone, but he was old and didn't have the hearing—not to mention the speed or strength—he used to, and he wouldn't be much help if the men came back in looking for trouble.

Rolling her eyes at herself, Katia cleaned up the table before sweeping and mopping. She was probably just letting her mind run away with her and seeing things that weren't there. The diner was physical work, but her job at the hotel left her far too much time to read crappy mystery and suspense novels when she wasn't studying.

She needed to lay off the mystery novels though, because her daydreams were leading her to believe that the men in the corner were Russian mafia.

Maybe she should switch to romance novels, instead.

Or, at the very least, stop listening to her uncle Sergei's tales of the old homeland, where he insisted her mother's family actually *had* been Russian mafia. She'd never believed it—although she had occasionally wondered just where Sergei's money came from, since he'd never worked for as long as she could remember—but she did indulge him when he liked to slip into storytelling mode. She'd always loved his accent, and she'd always loved a good story. It'd seemed like a win-win.

Now, when her mind was spinning ridiculous stories about the mob being in her diner, it didn't seem like much of a win.

Even though she told herself that her thoughts were ridiculous, she remained on edge, and she sped through the remaining work. All the prep had already been done, so other than sweeping and mopping, all that was left was counting the till down, which didn't take long at all.

After slipping the day's receipts into the office, she

locked it behind her and waited for Walt to join her before they headed out front. They always walked out together, but tonight she was more grateful than she usually was that she wasn't going out into the dark night alone.

Once she was in her car, she immediately locked the doors, watching as Walt started up his old car and pulled out before she followed him. She still felt uneasy, which was stupid as hell. If those guys really had been the Russian mob like she was imagining, then didn't that mean the diner, not to mention herself, were off limits? Her uncle owned it, after all.

Snorting at her thoughts, she pulled up to the bank, slipped the cash bag into the deposit slot on the wall, and honked at Walt as they parted ways. Her uncle wasn't the mafia, and neither were the guys in the diner. She really needed to get a grip on her overactive imagination.

She drove to the hotel, thankful it was in a slightly better area of town. Her uncle bought it about ten years ago, at the same time he bought the diner. He'd wanted to pay for her college tuition, but she didn't want to take any handouts. She wanted to work for what she had, so she compromised, letting him set her up in jobs at both businesses. He kept a portion of her paycheck to cover her room at the hotel.

He hadn't wanted to do any of it, but she refused to work for him or live at the hotel if he didn't. He'd grumbled for weeks about her being too stubborn for her own good, but he eventually gave in.

Hell, she probably *was* too stubborn, but she didn't want charity. Sergei raised her after her mom split when she was ten, and she already owed him for how generous he'd been with her. Most bachelors wouldn't want to take on the responsibility of an adolescent girl, but he'd stepped in without a complaint after her mom flaked, making sure she had everything she needed and most of what she wanted.

Exhaling, she shook herself out of her thoughts as she pulled to a stop and shut off the engine. Grabbing her purse, she walked to the door of the hotel, pausing with her hand wrapped around the handle as a strange sensation brushed down her spine.

It felt like someone was staring at her, and it was like a physical touch to her skin. It wasn't evil or sinister, but it still made the hair on her arms stand on end. Slowly turning, she scanned the semi darkened parking lot with narrowed eyes, but she didn't see anything suspicious.

There was a couple walking down the street on the other end of the lot, holding hands as they made their way to the restaurant next door. There were cars passing down the street, but no one else was nearby. That she could see, anyway.

Her eyes landed on a car parked in the corner, and she cocked her head as she stared at it. It looked like one that had been at the diner earlier, but there was no one in it, and no way to know for sure from this angle if it was the same one.

But surely it wasn't. There was no way the same

one belonging to the creepy men earlier was in the hotel's parking lot. That would be one hell of a coincidence, and she wasn't sure she believed in coincidences like that. Not after the way she let her imagination run wild earlier.

Shaking her head, she forced those thoughts out of her mind as she opened the door and slipped inside. What she needed was a long, hot shower, followed by about ten hours of sleep. Maybe then, she could get her imagination under control.

COLTON STRAIGHTENED WITH INTEREST AS A PRETTY brunette got out of her car at the hotel. She looked just out of place enough to pique his curiosity. It wasn't uncommon for people to be coming and going from a hotel, but one who was wearing what looked like a waitress uniform was.

He let his mind wander as she walked to the door, wondering what her story was. Was she coming to visit a friend? Maybe having trouble with something at her home, or even coming off of a break up, so she was staying at the hotel short term?

The truth really didn't matter, he supposed, but it was something to occupy his mind as he searched for any sign of Justin.

A moment later, she hesitated with her hand on the door, stiffening as she turned her head. He slid down in the truck seat, but her gaze passed right over him before coming to rest on the car parked in the corner. Eyes narrowing, he studied her as she froze, a hundred emotions flashing across her delicate features, too fast for him to pick any of them out.

He was just about to get out of the truck and ask her if she knew the car, or its owner, when she turned around and walked inside the hotel. Letting out a curse, he sat back in the seat, not willing to leave his spot long enough to chase her down. He couldn't risk leaving and missing Justin.

But knowing that he couldn't risk it didn't make it any easier for him to stay in his truck. That car was the closest lead he had to finding Justin, and if she knew anything about it, he needed to know. He wasn't going anywhere though, not unless his cousin showed up, so he'd be there when she came back out again.

Exhaling heavily, he scanned his surroundings again as his mind raced. But he was no closer to solving the riddle of what the hell was going on than he'd been in the beginning.

Everything had seemed fine for the last few months. Better than fine, actually. Better than it had been in years. When he first came back from Enforcer training, Justin tried to put on a normal, happy façade, but it wasn't long before it started to unravel.

It happened slowly at first, so slowly that Colton hadn't noticed it. Or maybe he'd been too selfish, so desperate to believe that things could go back to how they'd been before his cousin's dreams were crushed, that he willfully ignored the signs that not all was right.

Justin said that he'd known there was a chance he'd be rejected, after all. And Colton had gone to Enforcer training, just like his cousin asked—he hadn't finished, but Justin didn't know that. He'd enjoyed the training, more than he thought he would. But he couldn't shake the sense that he was training to work for blind idiots, and it'd been too weird without his cousin.

So, he'd packed up early and headed out, taking the long way home so Justin wouldn't know he bailed on completing the training. Like his dragon pointed out, he didn't want to make his cousin feel like he was keeping him from his dream.

Justin seemed a little down when he got back, but that was to be expected, so Colton decided to act like everything was fine, ignoring the signs that his cousin was cracking more and more with every passing day. After a year had gone by, he hadn't been able to ignore it any longer, but nothing he did or said helped. And the following five years hadn't gotten any better as Justin continued to spiral.

But then a few months ago, he completely turned around. He started showing signs of life again. Something had him excited and willing to try to live again, but no matter how much Colton pestered him, he wouldn't tell him what was going on.

And then he disappeared.

That was a month and a half ago and Colton hadn't rested since. Every second of his time was spent worrying, tracking, making call after call, trying desperately to find Justin. Just vanishing without a word wasn't like him. Even in his darkest moments, he found it in him to try to force a smile to reassure Colton. He wouldn't disappear without a trace, if for no other reason than he knew it would worry him.

Colton finally managed to track down a few people who saw him driving a black Toyota Camry with an Alabama tag and a Tasmanian Devil decal on the back corner of the windshield—just like the one in the corner of the parking lot.

Thanks to the help of a hacker he knew and a few illegal maneuvers, he finally tracked him to this area in Atlanta. He'd found the car at the hotel and went in to get a room for himself. But at some point, Justin slipped outside and left. Colton panicked and drove around in random circles looking for him, and when he finally gave up and came back here not too long ago, the car was back.

This time, he was staying in the damned truck until he set eyes on his cousin, no matter how long it took.

We'll find him, his dragon said, pacing with agitation inside him.

I know. At least I think I do. It's been too long.

I have a bond with his owl. He's still alive, and he's close. We will *find him.*

Colton shook his head, not replying. It was hard to stay hopeful like his dragon wanted, but he was trying. But whether he did or not, he knew he'd never give up, even if it looked completely hopeless. He'd scour the ends of the earth for his cousin for the rest of his life, if that was what it took.

It was times like this that he wished he'd become an Enforcer, though. That he had a team of badasses skilled in hunting at his back. Hell, he could have already found Justin if he had that.

For the millionth time, he thought about calling Blake Olsen. He'd gone through Enforcer training with him, and although they hadn't stayed close like they became during that grueling month of training, they stayed in touch. He knew Blake had an Enforcer team of his own, and knowing Blake as he did, they had to be the best of the best.

The only thing stopping him was that he'd found out the current mission the Blood and Bone Enforcers were on, and it was an important one. They'd found a male dragon who was kidnapping female dragons and auctioning them off. They were in the process of rescuing the females and taking Fernandez down—otherwise, Colton would have called them in ages ago.

But if he didn't set eyes on Justin—or at least hear from him—in the next week, he was calling them in, even if they were on an important mission.

Fucking entitled male dragons. They gave the whole species a bad name. They'd been taught from birth that they were superior in every way, that they had a right to everything. That if they saw something they wanted, they could just take it with no questions asked. And that included the females.

All dragons hid what they were. The majority of

people, shifters included, had no clue they even existed anymore. Dragon hunters used to roam the earth—they still did, although they were scarcer these days—hunting them down and killing them. Probably because they were a threat, and most people feared what they didn't know, especially anything that was more intimidating than them.

Kill them before they killed you. It was the number one rule of dragon hunters. They thought surely all dragons were evil man eaters, just waiting to devour them. And since there weren't any other shifter species capable of defeating a dragon in a fair fight, it painted a target on their backs.

Killing a dragon also gave someone bragging rights for life, since they were nearly indestructible in their animal forms. So not only did they have those who were scared hunting them, they also had idiots who wanted the title of Dragon Slayer.

Over time, their species had dwindled to few, and they were hovering on the brink of extinction. It didn't help that dragon babies were born few and far between. The women had difficulties getting pregnant, and the gene only passed through them. If a male dragon impregnated a different species, the child would always be the other animal. And if a female mated a different species, it was still rare for her to have a dragon baby.

That was why the females tried even harder than the males to hide. They didn't only have the hunters to worry about, they had the males, as well. Males were full of their own importance and their need to carry on their line, and they wouldn't hesitate to steal a female when they found her.

Fernandez wasn't just stealing them for himself, though. He was stealing them to auction them off to others and making himself a huge profit by doing so. The man was reprehensible scum.

Besides the situation with Justin, that was the only other time Colton yearned to be an Enforcer. He'd give anything to be on Blake's team, taking him down. His dragon hummed in agreement, and the sound sparked his ire more. He'd love to be there when they took him down, and he'd take pleasure in tearing him apart.

Because it didn't have to be this way. If each generation would stop teaching their children—the males, especially—that they were entitled to everything they wanted, the vicious cycle would end. The men might actually be fit to walk the earth, and the women wouldn't have to spend their lives fearing not only the hunters but their own species.

He was living proof that the old ways could be ditched. Maybe it was because his dad was a snowy owl, not a dragon. Colton was a rare breed—not only had his mom gotten pregnant with him, but he'd gotten her dragon and not his dad's owl. Or maybe because after his parents were killed, he went to live with his aunt and uncle, neither of whom were dragons. Regardless, it meant that being a dragon didn't mean they had to be total pricks.

Movement caught his eye and he jerked his head

around sharply, disappointment filling him when he saw it wasn't Justin. Blowing out a breath, he settled in to wait.

He wasn't going anywhere until he found his cousin.

Chapter 2

Yawning so wide she felt her jaw crack, Katia stood from her chair at the front desk, making her way to the coffee pot on the counter behind her. Despite her best efforts, it took her forever to fall asleep the night before, her mind too full of mysterious, creepy men to rest easily. She'd gone through half a pot already, but the jolts of caffeine didn't seem to be working very well.

She rushed to pour her cup, ready to sit back down as fast as she could. Her feet were still aching from the double shift the day before. Maybe she was getting too old to keep up the schedule she had. Snorting to herself, she took a long sip of coffee, not caring that it was still too hot to drink. It could burn her tongue all it wanted, so long as it woke her up a little.

Maybe she was working and studying too much. She felt a hundred years older than her twenty-six years. Sometimes she wished she didn't have such a strong work ethic and could have taken her uncle up on paying for college. It would have made life a lot easier, and she would have been done with school a long time ago, working one job in her chosen field.

Instead, she was working two jobs that weren't even close to being what she wanted to do with the rest of her life, and spending every other moment in class or studying. She was worn out, more tired than she should be, but she still didn't regret making the choices she had. She'd make them all over again if she had to.

Still... maybe it was time to try to carve out a few hours to find a real life. Maybe even go on a date every now and then. She couldn't remember the last time she'd gone on one. Years ago, she was sure.

But even if she wasn't dating, she needed to do something differently, shake up her life a little bit. Maybe then she'd have something else to occupy her thoughts than imagining strange men were the Russian mob.

The door to the hotel opened and she glanced over with an automatic smile, eyes widening as she saw the huge man walking inside. He was absolutely gorgeous, tall and muscled up as he sauntered through the lobby. He glanced her way and she swallowed hard as she met his striking hazel eyes. Grinning at her, he reached up and tipped the black cowboy hat he was wearing.

He walked toward the hallway opposite of the front

desk, and she couldn't tear her eyes away as she watched him. Her eyes traced over the length of him, stopping on his taut ass, highlighted to perfection in snug jeans.

She stared until he disappeared down the hallway, blowing out a breath and fanning her face. Lordy. They didn't get many men who looked like him in these parts, and she found herself wishing she'd been the one to check him in, so she knew his name.

Now, *he* was something worthy of daydreaming about, unlike the creepy dudes. If she'd seen him in the diner the night before, she probably still would have had a restless night, but hell, at least her dreams would have been a hell of a lot steamier.

A few moments passed by as she wondered just *how* steamy they would have been, but when she glanced up, it felt like she'd been doused with ice water. The men from the diner were walking into the lobby from the hallway opposite of the one the gorgeous cowboy went into, and she swallowed hard as her spine stiffened.

The car in the parking lot really had been theirs, then. Crap. It was a coincidence she didn't care for at all—and it had to be a coincidence. There was no way it was more than that. They walked toward the door and she dropped her eyes, pretending like she wasn't watching them while she gazed through her lashes. The one who paid their tab at the diner looked over at her, staring with narrowed eyes, and she gulped as her stomach tightened painfully.

She felt like a mouse that had just been spotted by a cat, but she didn't understand why she was reacting so strongly and negatively to these men. When she saw them at the diner, it was late at night after a long day of working, and she'd been tired. She could kind of understand it then.

But now... it was midmorning, and she'd at least gotten a little bit of sleep. She was still imagining them as sinister men, though, and her gut was telling her to run. Especially now that it seemed like that one had recognized her.

He finally looked away, leading the other one out as she gave a sigh of relief that was short lived as the other walked toward her. Plastering on what she hoped was a professional smile, praying that she didn't look like a scared deer caught in the headlights, she looked up fully as he made his way to the desk.

"I'd like to check out now," he said in a deep, cold voice. Was that a Russian accent she heard, or was she projecting things onto him that weren't there? "Room three fifteen."

Nodding, she accepted the room keys and tapped some commands into the computer, reading the name from the screen. "Certainly, Mr. Alexander. I hope your stay was a good one. Do you need a receipt?"

"No."

Eyebrows raising, she watched as he turned around abruptly and walked to the door. Once he was outside, she let out a sigh of relief as she slumped down in her chair. They'd checked out with no fuss and hadn't killed her for seeing too much before they left. She called that a win.

Snorting at the direction her thoughts went, she gazed at the keys, trying to resist the urge to go to their room and see if they'd left any incriminating evidence behind. Before she could give in to the urge, the hot cowboy from earlier walked back into the lobby. That time, she didn't spend the whole time he walked through staring at him, too distracted to give him the appreciation he deserved, but at least his presence distracted her from doing something stupid.

She should at least give the creepy men time to get on their way before she went snooping, after all.

Biting her lip, she waited about thirty seconds after the lobby emptied—the longest she was able to manage as curiosity burned through her—before picking up the key and standing. But before she could take a step, the door flew open as the cowboy rushed back inside. He jogged over to the desk, the friendly gleam in his hazel eyes replaced with panic.

"Did a man just check out? About my height, with brown hair and blue eyes. Did you see where he went?"

She felt her eyes widen as she stared at him, and she slowly her head. "I'm sorry, but I can't give you any information about guests—"

He cursed as his eyes dropped to the key in her hand. "He's gone, isn't he? Dammit!" Yanking his cowboy hat off, he ran his hand roughly over his brown hair before settling it back on. "What room was he in? I need you to let me in."

"I can't do that."

His eyes narrowed on her and she felt a shiver creep down her spine as his eyes turned from hazel to a shimmery, iridescent green and yellow. Was that—did his pupil just flicker and elongate for a second?

God, what was wrong with her? First, she imagined that men in the diner were in the mafia, and now she was seeing eyes flicker and change in a way no humans could.

Yeah. She definitely needed to get a life, because clearly all the time she spent working was beginning to make her hallucinate.

"I don't see why you can't. He's already checked out, right?"

"I'm not sure who you're looking for, but the man who just checked out was blond, so he can't be him. Is there something else I can do for you, Mister...?"

"Alexander," he muttered, still gazing at her with intense eyes, like he was trying to figure out the best way to talk her into doing what he wanted.

And then his last name registered, and her eyes dropped to the computer screen still pulled up. Justin Alexander. Uneasiness snaked through her belly as she realized they had the same last name.

Another coincidence? Somehow, she didn't think so.

. . .

COLTON NARROWED HIS EYES AT THE PRETTY BRUNETTE behind the desk—the same one he'd watched going into the hotel the night before. Actually, she was more than pretty. Gorgeous might not even be enough to describe her.

She had black hair that hung in loose curls to her shoulders, and sky-blue eyes that gazed up at him from a pixie face, with high cheekbones and full, kissable, bow shaped lips completing the package. She was much shorter than he was, the top of her head barely coming up to his shoulder.

If it wasn't for the panic rushing through his veins at the thought of missing his cousin—*again*—he'd be standing there hitting on her. But as it was, he couldn't afford to get distracted by a woman, no matter how beautiful she was.

He thought she had to know something more than she was letting on—the night before, she'd been staring at the car Justin was last seen driving, after all. And he was pretty sure his hunch was confirmed when he said his last name and her eyes widened before dropping to the computer screen.

"Listen," he said, leaning in as his eyes dipped to her name tag. "Katia, is it? This is important. My cousin, Justin Alexander, disappeared a month and a half ago. I've been tracking him ever since. The last car he was seen driving was sitting in the parking lot right before I came in, and now it's gone. If he checked out, you need to let me in the room. There could be a clue about where he's going next."

She swallowed hard, glancing down at the keycard she held in her hand before meeting his eyes again. "If he's missing, you should report it to the police and let them search for him."

"I'm sure they *are* searching," he fibbed, hoping he didn't look as uncomfortable as lying always made him feel. "But no one will look harder or more thoroughly than I will. I need to find him, Katia. Odds are that he didn't leave anything behind, but I need to see that for myself. Please."

Hesitating, she sank her teeth into her bottom lip as she gazed at him, a debate playing out in her sky-blue eyes. He hated when he had to lie to anyone, but for some reason it made him feel even shittier to do it to her.

But when it came to this, he had to. He couldn't involve law enforcement—not the human kind, anyway, and especially not without knowing exactly what was going on with Justin. Whatever he was wrapped up in, it could involve shifters. If that was the case, the last thing he needed to do was involve the human police.

It wasn't like he could tell Katia that, though.

She had a beautiful name—almost as beautiful as she was. He ran his eyes over her face, taking in her delicate features. She looked like she had Russian heritage, and her name fit her perfectly.

She exhaled, and he looked up to meet her light blue eyes. "Okay. But this is as much as I can help you. Don't ask to look at the records, or for his credit card number, or anything like that. This is as much as I'm willing to break the rules."

He hadn't even thought to ask about the credit card the hotel had on file. Some detective he was. It would be really helpful in his search—not that he knew how to track charges made to it, although his hacker friend might.

Katia cocked an eyebrow as she looked at him expectantly, and he reluctantly nodded. "I won't ask for anything else. I just want to see if he left anything behind."

"I can't believe I'm doing this," she muttered as she put a *back soon* sign on the desk and walked around the counter. "I'm not sure the guy who was in that room is your cousin, anyway. Like I said, he had blond hair. Maybe Justin's credit card was stolen."

"Maybe," he replied, considering that. But it would mean he'd been staked out at this hotel for nothing, and he didn't like the idea that he'd wasted his time. Besides, the car in the parking lot was the same one people said his cousin was driving. "Or maybe he dyed his hair or something."

She got in the elevator, hitting the button for the third floor as she looked at him dubiously. "Maybe. What's your first name?"

"Colton. Most people call me Colt, though."

"Well, Colt, I think this is a waste of time, but I still hope you can find something that will lead you to your cousin."

"I do, too. And I appreciate you letting me in, Katia."

She smiled at him faintly while giving him a nod as the elevator doors opened. Following behind her, his eyes dropped to her ass, highlighted in the snug jeans she was wearing, and he watched it as they walked down the hall. He couldn't pull his gaze away until they stopped at a door and she inserted the keycard. She really was a gorgeous woman, and he wished he'd met her under different circumstances.

Maybe once he found Justin, he'd make his way back here and try to get to know her better. It wasn't like he had much to go back to in Montana, anyway, besides the ranch he and Justin owned. But it always felt more like Justin's place than his, despite the fact that Colton's name was on the deed, too.

Yeah. He'd definitely have to see about coming back here and seeing Katia again.

His dragon rumbled with approval at the idea, and he quickly swallowed the sound down when Katia paused as she opened the door, glancing around with a frown. He did his best to smile innocently as her gaze landed on him, and her beautiful sky-blue eyes narrowed for a moment before she turned around and opened the door.

Quietly blowing out a relieved breath that she hadn't questioned the noise, he followed her inside, looking around with interest. At first glance, the room looked pretty tidy, but there could still be something inside that had a clue on it.

Katia moved farther into the room and he started to follow, but then halted abruptly when his dragon hissed inside him just as a coppery scent hit his nose. He narrowed his eyes on the closed bathroom door, dread welling up inside him as he wondered why the hell the smell of blood was coming from behind the door.

Inhaling deeply to steady his nerves, he grasped the doorknob and slowly pushed the door open. He walked in, flipping on the light as he went. His eyes went to the sink first and he froze, staring at the blood streaked in the basin. Whoever had been bleeding in here—and he suddenly hoped Katia was right and Justin's card was stolen, because he hated the thought that that might be his blood—they hadn't even tried to clean it up.

Taking a few steps forward, he slowly scanned the room, looking for any other hints of blood, rubbing his chest where his dragon was pacing furiously inside him. His animal was quiet, as he always became when he felt things too strongly, but Colton could feel his emotions.

He was furious, worried, and he was trying to hide it, but he was scared, too. Colton understood all the emotions all too well, because he felt the exact same way.

Taking a deep breath, he grimaced at the strong smell of blood as his gaze landed on the trash can. His blood ran cold as he noticed the bloody towels inside, and he steeled himself for what he might find as he grabbed a clean washcloth from the counter and bent to pick up the blood-soaked towels.

There was something tucked inside the towel, and he sat it on the counter to unwrap it, a curse slipping from his mouth when he saw the severed finger in the middle. Shit. What the hell was going on, and most importantly, whose finger was it?

Lord, please don't let it be Justin's. If it was, his cousin was in even more trouble than he'd thought.

"Hey, I found some papers in the trashcan in here," Katia called, her voice getting louder as she came nearer. "Maybe they can help you..."

He spun toward the door to stop her from coming inside and seeing the mess, but he was too late. Her voice trailed off as she came to an abrupt halt in the doorway, her wide eyes going to the sink and then the finger still sitting on its nest of bloodied towels.

"Is... is that a *finger*?" she asked faintly as the blood drained from her face, pausing to swallow hard. "Please tell me that's not real."

He slanted a look at the severed digit, shaking his head. "I wish I could."

"*Holy shit.* They really *were* the Russian mafia."

Chapter 3

Feeling queasier than she'd been in a long time, Katia tore her eyes away from the gruesome sight of the finger and bloody towels, turning to make her way back into the bedroom. Walking over to the table in the corner, she sank down onto one of the chairs and blew out a shaky breath.

What the hell had gone on in this room? She hadn't had any complaints of noise disturbances, and George, the night manager, hadn't mentioned getting any either when she first went on duty. But how could someone have their finger cut off and not scream fit to wake the dead?

"The Russian mafia?"

Glancing up, she watched Colton as he walked into the main room—sans finger, thankfully. Shrugging, she ran her hand through her curls as she shook her head.

"I mean, that was my first thought when I saw them in the diner last night, but I didn't honestly think I was right. I was positive my imagination was just running wild. Something felt off about them, though. I had a bad feeling in my gut, both last night when I waited on their table and then again when they checked out of here earlier."

There was still a part of her that was saying she was crazy to even entertain the thought that the creepy dudes were the mob—because that shit didn't happen in real life, right?—but there was a freakin' severed finger sitting on a pile of bloody towels in the bathroom that said she probably wasn't too far off the mark.

Maybe they weren't the mafia, but they were sure as hell Bad Guys with capital letters, so her gut hadn't been wrong when she saw them.

It was just so different from her normal, mind numbingly boring life that she hadn't been willing to entertain the thought that it was anything other than a combination of too many suspense novels, her uncle's crazy stories, and her own wild imagination.

Colton brought her attention back to the present as he sat on the edge of the bed, gazing at her intently. She took a moment to just drink him in, desperate to get her mind off how crazy her life had become in the space of the past twelve hours.

If there was ever anything that could make her

think about something other than what was sitting on the bathroom counter, it was him. God, he was gorgeous. She'd never thought she had a thing for cowboys before, but he was sexier than a man had a right to be, from his black cowboy hat all the way down to the worn boots on his feet.

His hazel eyes were still greener than she remembered them being when she first saw him, but at least she wasn't imagining that his pupils were elongating this time. He reached up a large, calloused hand, running it across the short brown beard on his face that perfectly highlighted his lips. The bottom was slightly fuller than the top, and they looked incredibly soft.

"Just how many jobs do you have, Katia?"

She blinked, coming out of the short-lived daydream she'd been starting to have about feeling those lips pressed against hers. Dammit. Now she was back in reality, where men like Colton didn't go around kissing women like her—and where there was someone's finger sitting a few feet away in the bathroom.

Her imagination always had been way better than her real life.

"I have two. Here and the diner. And I go to night school, too."

His eyebrows rose as he nodded slowly. "You're a busy woman. So, you saw them in the diner last night? Does that mean Justin wasn't alone? Who were the people he was with?"

Shrugging her shoulders helplessly, she shook her

head. "I don't know who any of them are. There were three of them, all men. They came in to eat last night, and I got a bad feeling about them right away. Two of them were keeping the third close to them. When they walked in and when they left, one of them kept his hand on the man's arm the whole time. It made me uncomfortable, but I tried my best to ignore them.

"I only looked at them directly when I took their order. I wanted to make sure the one they were keeping close wasn't in distress, and when I couldn't see any obvious signs, I kept my gaze away from them until one of them paid the tab. It was the same when they checked out earlier. This time, the other man paid, but the one who paid last night looked at me like he recognized me, and it creeped me out."

"You think maybe he *did* recognize you?"

She couldn't hold back a shudder. "I sincerely hope not."

"But you recognized the car they were driving, right?"

Cocking her head, she arched an eyebrow at him. "What makes you think I even saw what they were driving at all?"

He smiled sheepishly as he shrugged. "I was in the parking lot last night when you pulled up. I wanted to make sure I didn't miss Justin if he left. I saw you look over at the last car he was seen driving. A black Toyota Camry with an Alabama tag and a Tasmanian Devil sticker in the back window."

"Yeah, that was it. I felt like someone was watching

me—I guess that was *you*—and then I saw the car. I thought it looked like the one I saw them get into at the diner, but I didn't know for sure, since I couldn't see the plates from where I was."

Colton went quiet for a few moments, glancing at the bathroom door, and when he looked back at her, his greenish hazel eyes were full of worry and pain. Her heart clenched with sympathy as it hit her what finding the severed finger could mean for him.

All she'd been thinking about up until that point was how freaked out she felt, how nervous and scared, and it made her realize that she'd been being selfish. His cousin was missing, and he'd just walked into a hotel room rented in Justin's name to find someone had their finger cut off in there.

Either his cousin was one of the Bad Guys, which wasn't good, or he was now missing a finger and possibly in more danger, which was even worse. Regardless, in either case it was a shitty situation all around.

"Hey," she said softly, waiting until he met her eyes before continuing. "He might not have been here at all. He could have had his car stolen, and maybe his wallet was inside it when it happened. He might not even be in Atlanta at all."

He inhaled deeply and something passed quickly through his eyes, too fast for her to see what it was, as he shook his head. Opening his mouth, he paused, reaching into his pocket and pulling out his cellphone.

His thumb quickly swiped over the screen a few times before he handed it to her.

"This is Justin. Do you recognize him as any of the men you saw?"

Accepting the phone, she hesitated and took a deep breath before she looked down. She hated to be the one to give him any kind of bad news, but she knew if it was her cousin who was missing, she'd want answers, no matter what they were.

Finally making herself look, she studied the image on the screen. It was of Colton and the man she assumed was Justin, standing with their arms around each other's shoulders. Colton was grinning at the camera, his hazel eyes bright and his smile infectious. Justin was smiling too, but it wasn't as wide as his cousin's, and it didn't reach his blue eyes.

She studied it closely before handing the phone back to him. "He wasn't one of the threatening men, but I honestly can't tell you if he was the other one or not. He looks about the same size, but I didn't get a good look at the man the other two were leading around. He had a hat on, and he never once looked up or even gave me much of a profile view."

"I don't know whether to feel disappointed or relieved," he replied softly as he put his phone back in his pocket.

"I found a few receipts in the trashcan, but I don't think they'll be much help in figuring out where they went next."

He took them all from her and stuffed them into his pocket without looking at them as he stood. "Okay. We need to figure out what to do with that finger, and then we need to get out of here. We shouldn't have stayed as long as we did since they might have come back for something."

"Um, what do you mean, get rid of the finger? We need to call the police!"

"No, we don't," he replied grimly, pausing in the bathroom doorway to look back at her. "I can't really explain why right this moment, but I promise I will once we've put some distance between us and this hotel."

She felt her eyes widen as her mouth popped open, and disbelief flowed through her as she quickly stood and followed him to the bathroom. "Okay, first of all, what in the hell makes you think I'm going to leave the hotel with you? And second, the police can run the print off that finger, and then you'll know exactly who it belongs to. You'll know whether it's your cousin's, and if it's not, you'll know who he's with."

"You said they saw you here and at the diner. You even said one of them recognized you. And judging by this finger and all the blood, something bad went down here. You can identify them, Katia. They could decide to come back and take care of loose ends at any moment, and my gut says they will. You need to come with me, at least until this is over. I promise I'll protect you. No one can do it better than I can."

Biting her lip, she hesitated, torn. He actually had a good point with that. She was almost a hundred percent positive that one of them, at least, had recognized her as the waitress from the diner. It was possible that they took turns paying at different places to try to avoid anyone recognizing them, but they probably didn't count on visiting two different places with the same staff.

And maybe the only reason they hadn't already done anything about it was because it was daytime and there were too many potential witnesses around. They could plan on coming back after dark, or maybe they were still lurking, waiting on her to get off work so they could follow her home.

Either way, her gut said the same thing his did—they weren't done with her.

Shuddering, she wrapped her arms around herself as she gazed at Colton. "Maybe you have a point with that, but I'm not sure it's any safer to go off with a virtual stranger, either."

His mouth kicked up on one side. "If you have someone you can go to who's not related to you, that they won't be able to track you to, you're welcome to go there instead of coming with me. But I really do think you shouldn't come back to work at either job until this is over."

Sighing, she shook her head. "There's no one except my uncle, and everyone knows I'm his niece. Besides, I live here at the hotel and so does he, so whether I work or not, I'll still be here."

"All the more reason for you to come with me, then. You definitely can't sleep here with them knowing where to find you. I'd never hurt you, Katia. You have my word on that. You can also give my full name and address—hell, even my license plate number and a description of my truck—to anyone of your choosing. That way you'll have someone who knows exactly who you're with. But we need to hurry. We've already been here too long, and I really don't like that they know your name, what you look like, and where you work."

She didn't like it either, and that was finally what made up her mind. "Okay, but I'm giving my uncle all your information, and if anything happens to me, I'm gonna haunt your ass until he catches up to you and kills you himself."

"Fair enough," he replied with a half-smile. "Now go call whoever you need to so you can get your shift covered, but make sure they know to get here fast, because we're not sticking around to wait on them. Pack a bag, and once I'm done in here, I'll pack mine and we can meet in the lobby."

Nodding, she turned to go, pausing to look back at him. "You really should call the police, though. They can identify that finger and hopefully give you some answers about who it belongs to."

He froze and leaned in, staring intently at the severed digit. "I don't need to," he replied softly, his voice tight with emotion. His eyes were a kaleidoscope of green and yellow when he glanced over at her, and the pain she saw inside them stole her breath. "It's

Justin's. He had a birthmark in the shape of a star on his right index finger—same as the one on this one."

Her heart squeezed as compassion filled her. "I'm so sorry, Colt."

Clearing his throat, he shook his head as his hands clenched tightly. "He's still alive, and that's what counts. And I'll make those motherfuckers pay when I find them. Now go do what you need to do so we can get out of here."

Nodding, she turned without saying anything else, pulling her phone out of her pocket to call her uncle as she went to her room. She'd really been hoping that his cousin hadn't been at the hotel at all. Or, if he had been, that one of the Bad Guys had somehow lost a finger and not him.

She'd never met Justin, and maybe it was because she'd seen how much Colton cared for him and how worried he was, but the thought of him being in so much trouble made her heart hurt. And she hoped that nothing else happened to him before he could be found. It was clear that Colton loved him very much, and she instinctively knew that it would devastate him if he lost him.

Maybe it was stupid of her, but she wasn't the least bit afraid of going off with someone she just met. Mostly because it didn't *feel* like they'd just met—it felt like she'd known him for years. Besides, the gut that so correctly warned her that the Creepy Dudes were bad news was also telling her Colton was trustworthy, so she was going to roll with it until he proved otherwise to her.

But she was damned sure going to give Sergei all his info, just in case her gut was wrong this time.

Colton walked back into the hotel, his gut churning. He had a sick feeling in his stomach the moment he saw the finger, and he'd suspected it was Justin's. His cousin's scent had been all over the room, so he'd known as soon as he walked in that he'd been there—even though, for a moment, he tried to convince himself Katia was right that maybe Justin hadn't been—and there was no way he'd just sit around and allow someone else's finger to be cut off. But suspecting it was his was absolutely nothing like seeing the birthmark and knowing for sure it whose finger it was.

He hadn't wanted to wrap it in colored plastic and throw it in the dumpster either, but he hadn't known what else to do with it. It made him a little sick to just throw it away, but he couldn't hold onto it. He just hoped no one found it, and that he'd done a good enough job on the cleanup in the bathroom.

If the blood or finger were found and then tested, they'd know that Justin was more than human, and he couldn't let that happen. Shifters kept their existence a closely guarded secret. As far as he knew, his cousin's prints weren't in any systems, but he didn't want to take the chance that the blood could be traced back to him, or that they'd find DNA that shouldn't exist in it.

That would put *all* shifters in danger.

He couldn't believe he was even contemplating this shit, and he fucking hated the reason he had to. He'd known something was seriously wrong from the moment Justin disappeared, but seeing his severed finger drove it home with sickening clarity.

When he found the men who did this, he was going to kill them.

You kill them, I'll burn the bodies, and then we'll dance around their ashes while we celebrate, his dragon rumbled inside him, his voice fierce with the longing to do just that.

You bet your ass we will, Colton replied, vowing to do everything in his power to make that a reality.

He wasn't normally so bloodthirsty, and neither was his dragon. His animal was a gentle giant, despite what he was. But they both had protective streaks a mile wide—which was part of why they wanted to be Enforcers back in the day—and they turned fierce when someone they considered theirs was threatened.

And that was even more true for Justin, who was like a brother to him, not to mention his best friend. Which was what made his decision to get Katia out of the city instead of immediately trying to track them down the hardest decision he'd ever fucking made.

His heart literally hurt at the thought of leaving Justin to fend for himself longer, when God only knew what was happening to him, and a heavy knot of dread was coiled tightly in his stomach. But he couldn't leave Katia in danger, either—and his gut was one hundred percent certain that at least one of those fuckers was nearby, waiting for his opportunity to strike and get rid of the woman who could identify them.

She was a complete innocent in this, and Colton couldn't let her be hurt or even killed just for being in the wrong places at the wrong times. All she was guilty of was having two jobs and working too hard, and she didn't deserve what came from being the unfortunate person to see them twice.

And whether he wanted to admit it or not, whatever mess Justin was in... well, he chose it. Maybe he didn't choose to be captured—or whatever the hell happened to land him with those fuckers—or to get his finger cut off, but he got himself into this situation. He'd been up to something for months before he disappeared, and he made a conscious decision to vanish without telling anyone where he was going or what he was doing.

But that didn't mean making the decision to get Katia to safety *before* rescuing Justin from whatever mess he was in—and risking the possibility of losing him forever—wasn't painful as fuck. Especially knowing he was being hurt and possibly tortured, and that every moment he was with those bastards was another moment when his life could be ending.

You're doing the right thing, his dragon said quietly.

Am I? he asked, clenching his hands tightly into fists. *Scratch that. I know I am, and I know I wouldn't be able to live with myself if something happened to her. Especially since it would be a direct result of me and Justin barging into her life. But not immediately tracking Justin down feels all kinds of wrong, and like a betrayal to the man who's basically a brother to me.*

You know how much I love Justin. I need to find him as much as you do. But like you said, he got himself into it, and she's an innocent in all this. Besides, he's a grown man skilled in fighting, and he's a shifter on top of that. He stands a better chance against them than she does.

Exhaling quietly, he nodded, acknowledging that point. *You're right, of course. It's just a shitty situation all around.*

That it is. His dragon went quiet inside him for a moment. *Is that the only reason you don't want anything to happen to Katia?*

He frowned, something stirring inside him uneasily. *What are you getting at?*

I'm just saying, you've never reacted to a woman as strongly as you did to her. Maybe you're too distracted by everything going on to recognize it, but I can tell how much you like her.

An image of her sky-blue eyes and pixie face flashed through his mind, and he nodded with a quirk of his lips that quickly faded. *You're right, I do. If I'd met her at any other time, I would have immediately asked her out. As it is, though, I feel guilty for even thinking about anything other than finding Justin right now.*

I don't think you have anything to feel guilty about. If you were abandoning the search in order to pursue her, that would be one thing, but you're not. I don't see anything wrong with getting to know her while she's with you.

Nodding slowly, he considered that. Maybe his dragon was right. He didn't know if he'd ever feel right about enjoying himself—and he couldn't kid himself that he wouldn't be doing just that as he got to know her—while his cousin's life was in jeopardy. But he already knew he wouldn't be able to pass up the opportunity to get to know her better while he had the chance.

When he got to his room, he set to work packing his bag. It didn't take long at all, considering that he hadn't even had a chance to sleep in the room. He'd gotten there the day before but ended up dozing fitfully in the truck the night before, unable to fall asleep fully while he watched for his cousin—only to have Justin leave when he went in to use the bathroom and get his phone charger.

But even though he was done quickly, it still felt like it took too long. He'd love nothing more than to run into the soon-to-be-dead fuckers who had Justin, but he didn't want them anywhere near Katia.

He might have strong protective instincts, but it was surprising how deeply he felt it for her. He didn't normally feel it like this for anyone he'd just met—but with her, keeping her safe wasn't just a want, it was a *need*.

It was probably just because the men he was trying to protect her from were the same ones who had Justin, and it was clear at this point how little they cared about hurting someone. But whatever the reasons he felt it so strongly, he'd be damned before he let anything happen to her.

He was really glad she agreed to come with him with hardly any fuss, because he'd been determined to get her out of there, no matter what. And there was no denying that it made life infinitely easier that she was coming willingly, rather than him forcing her.

Because as much as he hated the thought of forcing her to do anything, he would have in this case. He'd do anything to keep her safe—and he was going to come back to that and examine why he felt that need so strongly as soon as she was out of immediate danger, and he could spare his thoughts and energy on it.

Striding into the lobby, he looked around for her, brow furrowing when he didn't see her right away. He walked a few more steps inside, his frown easing when he saw her head pop up from behind the desk as she straightened.

Glancing up, she spotted him and smiled, knocking the breath right out of him. Damn, she was so gorgeous. He couldn't help wishing that they'd met under completely different circumstances, and he made a silent promise that as soon as this was over and Justin was back home where he belonged, he was going to devote the time and energy to getting to know her that she deserved.

"Are you ready?" he asked, clearing his throat when his voice came out husky.

She nodded, walking around the counter, and he

took her bag out of her hands, motioning for her walk to the door. "Thanks. Yeah, I was just checking you out of your room. I figured you might not be back for a while, and you don't need a bunch of nights charged to your card when you're not even staying here."

"That was a good idea. Thanks," he replied absently, running his gaze over her. She'd pulled on a hoodie that was about three sizes too big, and it hung off her small frame. He figured she'd done it so that if the men were still there, it would throw them off and they wouldn't recognize her.

Maybe it would be enough to fool them, but Colton thought he'd recognize her anywhere—but that was probably just him. The awareness he felt when she was nearby was incredible.

He stopped by the door, watching as she pulled the hood over her head. "Putting that on is a great idea, but I'm still going to get my truck and drive it up to the door. Hop in as soon as I come to a stop, but don't pull the hood off until we're well on the way, okay?"

She nodded, her sky-blue eyes serious, and he put both bags in one hand as he pulled out his keys. Walking swiftly to his truck, he put them in the backseat and got in, wincing at the loud growl of the exhaust as he started the engine. He loved the way his truck looked and sounded, and he'd put a lot of time, effort, and money into getting it just how he wanted it, but that and the lift kit he'd had put on made it a little hard to blend in.

He never had any clue he'd need to though, and sure as fuck not for this reason.

As soon as the truck came to a stop, Katia climbed in, pulling off her backpack before buckling her seatbelt. He was moving before she even had it fastened, brow twitching as he realized he didn't have any idea where to go next, other than getting her away from the hotel and out of the city entirely.

He turned toward the interstate, thinking he'd figure out where they were going once he'd put some distance between themselves and the men who'd be looking for her. He really did believe that they'd most likely come back for her at some point—or hell, maybe they never even went far from the hotel at all and were waiting for her to leave so they could follow her home.

As he drove, his mind raced as he tried to figure out what the hell was going on. What could Justin have gotten mixed up in that caused him to lose a finger? Try as he might, he couldn't figure it out.

Yeah, there'd been something up with him for the last few months before he disappeared, but whatever it was, he'd been excited about it. How'd he go from being happy and excited to being held captive and tortured?

Once they were on the interstate, Katia pulled her hood off and reached into her backpack, pulling out a sketchpad and pencils. He glanced over as she pulled a leg up on the seat and opened the pad, flipping quickly through the pages until she found a blank one.

"You draw?" he asked, wishing he'd gotten a better look at her work.

"Yeah. I've always loved it, and one of the classes I take at night school is an art class."

"Is that what you're going to school for?"

She laughed, the sound light and wistful at the same time. "I wish. If there was a way to make a living off it, I'd do it in a heartbeat. I'm an advertising major, but I'm hoping I get to use my art in campaigns once I have a job in that field."

He glanced over at her, watching as her pencil flew across the page before looking back at the road. "How long have you been working two jobs and going to school?"

"I've been working at the diner since I was seventeen, and I started at the hotel after I graduated high school. I didn't start taking classes until I was twenty, though. I wanted to try to save up some money to pay for it first. I've been in school for six years now, because I can't take nearly as many classes as a full-time student, but I only have eight months left."

Eyebrows raising, he slanted another glance at her. "That's impressive. How'd you come to live at the hotel?"

Her hand stilled as she looked over at him with a wry smile. "My uncle Sergei owns it. He wanted to pay for my tuition and get me an apartment, but I was stubborn and wanted to do it on my own. I took jobs at his diner and hotel instead, and insisted he take a portion of my paycheck to cover the room. He doesn't charge me nearly as much as he should, but it was a decent compromise between what we both wanted."

"What about your parents? They didn't offer to help?"

"I never knew my dad, and my mom skipped out when I was ten. She calls Sergei every now and then, so I know she's alive, but I never have any interest in talking to her. He raised me after she left, and he did a damn good job of it. Better than she ever did. But he didn't ask for any of that, and he didn't have to step up like he did. I felt like I owed him. I still do, honestly, and I don't want to take anything more from him."

Compassion and admiration welled up inside him. She'd been dealt a rough hand at a young age, but she hadn't let it slow her down. She was working hard to fight for her dreams, and she wanted to do it all by herself, with help from no one.

"Your uncle sounds like a good man."

"He's the best," she replied with a soft smile. "Although I'm starting to think I listened to his stories about the mafia in his homeland a little too often."

"Is that where your Russian mafia comment came from?"

She shrugged wryly as she laughed. "Yeah. I grew up listening to those stories. Even before my mom flaked, I was with Sergei more than her. He's her brother, and he swore their family in the homeland is the mob. I enjoyed listening because I loved his accent and the stories are always entertaining.

"It was a combination of those stories and the

mystery and suspense novels I read that made me think the guys in the diner were the Russian mafia. I told myself it was stupid, but my gut said they were creepy and Bad Guys, and I couldn't make myself shake the thought."

Arching an eyebrow, he glanced over at where she was still sketching away. "Why do I get the impression that you just capitalized *bad guys* like it's an official title?"

Katia laughed again, the light sound sheepish. "Because I do in my head. That and Creepy Dudes. It's weird, I know, but I feel like they deserve it as a title."

Colton chuckled as they fell quiet, and he concentrated on driving while she went back to her drawing. Not only was she beautiful, but he found himself drawn to her personality. She was charming and funny, and she was strong as hell.

How many women could come face to face with evil, set eyes on a bloody, severed finger—and then on top of all that, have a complete stranger steal her away because her life was now in danger, all without losing her shit?

Most women—hell, most men too—that he knew would be hysterical at this point, but she was holding it together like a champ.

She's a remarkable woman, his dragon said as the furious pacing he'd been doing since Justin went missing slowed while he contemplated her. *If I didn't know better, I'd say she was a shifter—maybe even a dragoness. She's got enough strength to be one.*

Pursing his lips, Colton nodded slowly. *The only female dragon I was ever around was my mother, and I don't remember her well, but I think you're right. Katia is as amazingly resilient as I imagine my mother was.*

He glanced over at her, watching as she bit her lip in concentration while she sketched. Warmth filled his chest, catching him off guard, and he quickly turned his attention back to the road.

Brow furrowing, he wondered where the hell that sensation came from, and whether he liked it or not. Hell, who was he trying to kid? He enjoyed the hell out feeling it, and he knew if he was going to feel it for anyone, there wasn't anyone better than her.

But the timing fucking sucked, because until he found Justin, there wasn't a damned thing he could do about it. All of his focus needed to be on keeping her safe and bringing his cousin home, and he couldn't afford to be distracted from those goals.

And wasn't that just his fucking luck.

Chapter 4

Blinking as she came out of the zone she fell into when she drew, Katia lowered her pencil as she gazed at the passing scenery. A sign caught her eye and her eyebrows rose as she turned to look at Colton.

"We're in Tennessee?"

The corners of his mouth curled up as he glanced at her. "Just now noticed that, did you? Yeah, for about thirty minutes now."

"Are we going somewhere in particular?"

"No. I honestly didn't have a plan when we left the hotel. I just wanted to put some distance between us and them. I'm going to stop at the next exit though, and we'll figure it out then."

Nodding, she fell quiet as he slowed down and exited the interstate. He drove to a gas station and once he was parked, she opened the door, thankful he had step sides on the truck as she got out. She was way too short to climb in and out of the jacked-up truck without them.

Walking around as he filled the gas tank, she stretched out her legs and back, eyes narrowing on a car that slowed like it was going to turn in the parking lot before continuing on the road. Suspicion rose inside her, but she brushed it off as she strolled. It wasn't the Camry the Creepy Dudes were driving, so it was probably just an idiot who couldn't decide where he was going.

"Want anything to drink?"

"A Coke, please," she replied, watching as he nodded and walked inside.

Damn, he looked good. His stride was fluid and graceful, despite how big he was, and her eyes fell to the taut globes of his ass, watching as they moved with his steps. She felt damned near mesmerized, unable to look away until he disappeared inside.

Blowing out a breath, she fanned her face as she made her way back to the truck. She didn't think she'd ever seen a man as gorgeous as Colton in real life, and she honestly wasn't sure how she'd managed to ignore his presence long enough to finish her sketches.

It was too bad they met under these circumstances. What she wouldn't give to have met him in a normal setting, to be with him right now because they were maybe on a date—not because his cousin disappeared, and he was trying to keep her safe from the men who had him.

The warmth that had been building in her belly as she watched him dissipated, turning to a heavy knot of dread and fear. Suddenly feeling chilled down to her bones, she wrapped her arms around herself, shuddering as an image of the severed finger flashed through her mind.

This whole situation was fucked up and it felt so surreal. How did she go from her pathetically boring life, longing for something more to happen than just going to work and school, and spending every spare moment studying—to this?

She'd wished for something to happen that would shake up her life a little, but she hadn't wanted her whole existence to turn upside down, and definitely not for this reason. When the Bad Guys walked into the diner the night before, it started a domino effect that was still in motion, with no signs that it was going to slow down any time soon.

First having the horrible misfortune of being able to identify the creeps, and then seeing that finger. And now fleeing from everything she knew and was familiar with in order to stay safe—and the whole time, even when she was zoned out as she sketched, there was a lump in her throat and a ball of fear in her gut.

Katia shook her head, disgusted with herself. There she was, being selfish again. Because she knew as hard as the situation was on her, it was a million times worse for Colton. His cousin went missing and then he found out that the men he was with had cut off his finger, and Lord only knew what else they'd done to him. He had to be worried out of his mind.

And poor Justin... there was no telling what he'd been through, what he was going through in that very moment.

Out of the three of them, she had it the best in their situation, and she resolved to stop feeling sorry for herself. She'd made strides in trying to help out on the drive, but she was going to do whatever it took to do more.

At first, she'd hoped Colton was taking her somewhere she could hide out while he continued to look for Justin. But she made up her mind then and there to stick to him like glue until everything was over so she could help.

Maybe it was because it felt like she was living in a movie and none of this was real, but as soon as she made the decision, determination replaced the fear in her stomach. Inhaling the first deep breath she'd been able to take since she saw the finger, she glanced over as the door to the store opened and Colton emerged.

Her breath caught as she watched him walking toward her, cowboy hat perched firmly on his head and a smile directed her way. Butterflies teased her belly, and she decided that rather than viewing this as a horror movie like she had been, she was going to pretend it was a romance.

Maybe it would help her keep the fear of their

reality at bay—she just had to make sure she didn't forget that this wasn't truly a love story. Viewing it that way was probably one of the stupider ideas she ever had, but that was okay as long as it helped her overcome her fear to do what was right.

Instead of rushing after the Creepy Dudes who had his cousin right away and rescuing Justin, Colton got her the hell out of Dodge first to keep her safe—possibly costing him the opportunity to find them quickly. Didn't she owe it to him to help him?

The guilt welling up inside her over the fact that she could be the reason Justin was hurt worse, while she herself was perfectly safe, said she sure as hell did.

Walking over to the truck, her eyebrows rose as she saw him opening her door for her. She put her foot on the step side and started to smile as he put one of the drinks down, cupping his big hand around her arm to help her inside.

But in the next moment, her smile faded as the warmth of his hand sunk into her, and she sucked in a breath as she felt her eyes widen.

Good Lord Almighty, what was *that*?

It felt like a bolt of electricity arched from his hand to her skin, and tingles raced down her arm, goosebumps raising the hair on her arm in its wake. Swallowing hard, she tried to compose her expression before he could see just how shaken she was.

Had he felt that too, or was she a little *too* good at pretending this was a romantic movie?

Settling into her seat, she inhaled shakily as she

searched his eyes for any hint that he was as off balance as she was. "Thank you," she whispered, not able to give her words any substance.

He nodded silently, his hazel eyes seeming to turn greener as she gazed into them. He was searching her eyes intently, like he was looking for confirmation of his own, and it made her think that maybe—just maybe—he'd felt it, too.

"You're welcome," he replied huskily, stopping to clear his throat. "I would have done it earlier, but we were in a hurry."

Nodding, she watched as he closed her door and walked around to his side, not taking her eyes off him until he climbed inside. Handing her the Coke, he started the truck but only went as far as the parking lot of the hotel next door.

Puzzled, she glanced at the clock to find it was only four in the afternoon before looking over at him. "What are we doing?"

"I figured this is as good a place as any to stop for the night and work out a plan. We need to figure out where we're going next before we keep driving."

Narrowing her eyes, she started to protest, but he was out of the truck and getting their bags before she could. She didn't think they needed to stop for the whole night, but he was right when he said they needed a plan.

Shoving her sketchpad into her backpack, she zipped it up just as he opened her door and held his hand out for her. Curious to see if the spark happened again, she placed her hand in his, butterflies exploding in her stomach as electricity raced over her skin.

His hand tightened around hers and her eyes flew up to meet his shimmery green and yellow gaze. His eyes dipped to her lips for a moment and when he met hers again, the heat she saw made her glad she was still sitting down as her knees weakened.

Katia inhaled deeply, willing herself to break eye contact long enough to find the strength to get out of the truck. It took longer than she thought possible, and the whole time, both of them stood completely still, locked in each other's eyes.

It was a passing car honking its horn that finally did it, and she quietly blew out a breath as she stepped down. They were quiet as they went inside, and her mind was swirling with so many thoughts and questions that she forgot to stop him from renting a room.

"I hope you don't mind that I only got one room," he said quietly as he led her to the elevators, his deep voice caressing her nerve endings. "I don't want to take the chance that we were followed, though, and leave you to fend for yourself. I got two beds, and I promise to stay in mine. You're safe with me."

Well, that was a damned shame.

For one horrifying moment, she feared she said the thought out loud, but when she risked a glance up at him, he gave no indication that she had. Breathing a sigh of relief, she followed him to the room in silence.

When they were inside, she set her backpack on one of the beds before saying what she'd meant to earlier. "I agree that we need to figure out a plan, but we didn't need to stay the night to do that."

Shrugging, he put their bags down and sat on the edge of the other bed. "I thought it was for the best, and we can get a fresh start first thing in the morning. Besides, I didn't sleep very much at all last night. I was too busy looking for Justin. I didn't want to miss him if he checked out."

"You spent the night in your truck?" she asked, eyebrows high. "But you had a room at my hotel."

"Like I said, I didn't want to miss him. When I checked in, I put my stuff in my room and when I came back out, the car was gone. I panicked and drove around in circles, and when I got back, the car was there again. I didn't want to risk missing him for good the next time."

A fresh wave of guilt washed over her, and she exhaled softly as she sank down onto her bed, facing him with their knees almost touching. "And you ended up missing him for good anyway, because of me."

Brow twitching, he immediately shook his head. "Technically, I missed him when I ran inside to use the bathroom and get my phone charger. He'd already left by the time I got back out there. You had nothing to do with it."

"I still feel like it's my fault, though. If I'd let you into his room sooner, or not freaked out and needed calming down, you might have been able to catch up to them."

"You were following the rules by not letting me in,

and I would have thought there was something wrong with you if you weren't disturbed by what you saw. You did nothing wrong, Katia."

Hesitating, she sank her teeth into her bottom lip as she glanced at her folded hands. Maybe he had a point with that, but it didn't stop her from feeling like she'd screwed everything up—just by virtue of being there. If she'd only worked at one of those places that day, maybe her involvement could have been avoided, and he could be tracking his cousin right now.

Praying for courage, she inhaled deeply as she looked back up into his eyes. "I think we should go back to my hotel."

He frowned as he shook his head. "No way, not this soon. I told you that you needed to stay away from there until this was over. They could still be in the area watching for you."

"Exactly. It gives you the perfect opportunity to find your cousin and take care of the assholes who have him."

He cocked his head as he studied her, and then his frown deepened. "Tell me you're not suggesting I use you as bait."

Narrowing her gaze, she studied his eyes closely. There for a moment, it looked like his pupils flickered and elongated before shrinking back down to normal. She thought she was hallucinating from stress or something the first time she saw it—although that was a weird as hell thing to imagine—but why would she do it twice?

It didn't make any sense at all.

Filing it away to puzzle over later, she refocused on Colton. "That's exactly what I'm suggesting."

"Have you lost your mind?" he asked, voice saturated with disbelief. "You saw what they're capable of, Katia. And that was probably just the tip of the iceberg. Yet you want to put yourself right back in their crosshairs."

"Do you any better ideas for finding Justin? If you had some way to track him, you wouldn't have slept in your truck, so you didn't lose him. If I go back to work and they're watching me, you can be there to get answers."

Mouth tightening, he shook his head. "It's way too fucking risky."

"You'll be there to protect me and keep them from actually getting to me. I'll be fine. And then you can get one of the bastards and make him tell you where your cousin is."

"It's still a no."

Narrowing her eyes, she blew out a breath with exasperation as she contemplated how to get him to agree. She hadn't really expected him to fight her on her plan, especially since he could find his cousin if they went back—but he wasn't even willing to consider it.

Despite the frustration she felt that he wasn't giving this more thought, her heart still warmed over his resistance. The only person on the planet who'd ever cared about her safety and what happened to her was her uncle Sergei. Lord knew, her mom never really had, and she didn't remember her dad at all, since he left when she was still a baby.

Yet there Colton was, sitting across from her looking more delicious than a man had a right to, refusing to do the one thing that they knew could get his cousin back. She'd sensed right from the start how much he cared for Justin, and the fact that he was willing to put her safety first...

Well, there were no words for it. But she felt all warm and fuzzy inside.

She felt cared for.

It was such a foreign feeling that she almost wasn't sure what to do with it, but she was going to bask in it for as long as he was still around. And she'd treasure it long after he was gone.

The thought that there was a limit on their time together made her stomach drop, and she forced herself to focus on the conversation, and convincing him that they needed to go back.

"I know not immediately following after Justin is tearing you up inside," she said softly. "Don't try to deny it, because I can see it in your eyes. You're sure they were going to come back for me to silence me, and I agree with you. Going back is the perfect plan. They'll see me and it'll draw them out, and you'll get them before they get me. Then you can finally get your cousin back, and I know that means everything to you."

. . .

COLTON

Colton stared at Katia, unable to find words to reply just yet. He'd known she was beautiful, charming, and strong—but now he had to add brave to the list. She was willing to put herself right in the path of danger so he could rescue Justin, and she didn't even know his cousin.

He searched her light blue eyes, searching for any clue as to her motivation. Maybe he was misreading it, but he swore he saw a little gleam of affection and warmth for him. Was she willing to go back into such a dangerous situation for *him*?

It fit with what she said about seeing the worry in his eyes, and that she knew getting Justin back meant everything to him. But it was still hard to wrap his mind around.

He snorted to himself, wondering when he became so arrogant. Maybe that was part of her reasoning, but he was sure it wasn't all of it, or even half of it. She was a hell of a woman, and he didn't think she ever put herself first. If she did, she would have taken her uncle up on his offer to pay her tuition and get her an apartment the moment he made the offer.

She wasn't the type of person to be content with letting her own safety be put in front of someone else's. He wasn't sure why he was so certain that was the case, but he was, and it fit everything he'd learned about who she was since they met.

Didn't mean he was going to take her up on her offer though, no matter how much he burned with the need to find Justin and get him to safety.

"Colt?"

Blinking, he surfaced from his thoughts to find her staring at him with an arched eyebrow and a question in her beautiful eyes. "You're right, of course. I do want to find him and make sure he's okay. I want it with every fiber of my being, Katia. But just as much as I want that, I want to keep you safe. I *need* to. Your safety's just as important to me as Justin's, and I'm not willing to risk it. Besides, your plan has a major flaw. I don't even know what the men look like, so I'd have no idea when they were approaching you."

She gazed at him with wide eyes, looking like she wasn't even breathing. She slowly shook her head, but he thought it was more in disbelief than denial. Clearing her throat, she glanced away as she inhaled deeply, and then looked at him with a wry smile.

"I appreciate that you value my safety so much, Colt. I can't even put into words how much, and I'm incredibly thankful that you're trying to look out for me. You're wrong about one thing, though."

"Oh, yeah? What's that?" he asked, cocking an eyebrow.

Katia didn't reply as she reached for her backpack. Opening it, she pulled out her sketchpad and flipped through the pages, handing it to him silently. Curious to finally see her work, he took it from her, surprise filling him as he looked at the drawing.

A man's face filled the page, all the detail in the image making it look so lifelike, it felt more like he was looking at a picture taken with a camera than a drawing.

"Katia, this is amazing," he said softly, glancing up quickly before he went back to studying it.

"Thanks. Turn the page and look at the other one."

He did as she suggested, finding another man and taking in all the details in the drawing that was just as good as the first. Eyes narrowing as he noticed how cold the man's eyes were, he flipped back to the other one and saw he had the same hard gaze.

"What are these?" he asked slowly, flipping back and forth between them.

"Those are the men who had your cousin. So you see, we do know what they look like."

He looked up to meet her eyes, his blood turning to ice in his veins. "These are them?"

She nodded. "Down to the last detail, from the mole on creep one's cheek to the scar on creep two's chin. I tried to ignore them as much as possible, but I got a few good looks in, and I never forget a face. I think it's the artist in me. I always notice all the details so I can recreate the things I see in my drawings."

Nodding, he glanced back down, studying each drawing closely again, committing the faces to his memory. It was helpful to know what they looked like, so he didn't accidentally kill the wrong people when the time came.

And we will definitely kill these sons of bitches, his dragon hissed, practically breathing fire inside him.

Bet your ass we will.

"Thanks for drawing these. Knowing what they look like is definitely helpful."

"So now that you'll be able to recognize them, can we go back?"

He snorted, resisting the urge to look at her other drawings as he closed the sketchbook and handed it back to her. "Not likely. My other reasons still stand. Why are you so anxious to put yourself back in danger?"

Shrugging, she twisted her fingers together. "I want to help you and Justin. And I really don't like that he's still stuck with the Bad Guys because you rushed me away to safety. I'm not a damsel in distress, but I've done nothing except act like one since I met you. Besides, I have absolutely no doubts that you'll do your best to protect me. I have complete faith in that."

His breath caught at the complete conviction in her voice and sky-blue eyes, and he cleared his throat, searching for words. The only person who'd ever had that much faith in him was Justin. His aunt and uncle had been kind, but while they'd always taken care of him, they were also distant, with both him and their son.

That was probably why they'd grown so close so quickly growing up. They were each other's support system, and no one believed in him more than Justin.

But now there was a gorgeous woman with a heart of gold entrusting him with that same amount of faith, and he felt humbled beyond measure that she thought he was worthy of it. And he was determined to make sure her trust wasn't misplaced.

"What if my best isn't good enough in this case?" he asked, his words coming out hoarse.

There was pure confidence in her voice when she replied. "I *know* it is. I can see the desire and need to protect me and find your cousin shining from your eyes. It's so strong, I can practically feel it down in my soul." Pausing, she blushed, her cheeks turning a pretty shade of pink. "That probably sounded more dramatic than I meant it to, but it's still true. And I already know you're not a man who lets anything stand in his way when he decides to do something."

He swallowed hard as emotions overwhelmed both him and his dragon. Awe, gratefulness, resolve to protect her no matter what—and something else he wasn't sure he could identify. He ran his eyes over her, taking in her tousled black curls, light blue eyes, perfectly bowed lips, and then down her small frame, trying not to linger on the way her breasts filled out her V-neck top.

The urge to stare was strong as desire washed over him, but he forced his gaze down to her red painted toenails before retracing the journey. He met her eyes, taking in the faith and trust shining from the blue depths, still trying to figure out what else he was feeling.

Whatever it was, it was strong enough to steal his breath, and it seemed to be affecting his dragon the same way.

Realizing he'd been quiet for too long when she raised a delicately arched eyebrow, he cleared his throat as he searched for words. "I can't tell you how much your faith in me means, Katia. Justin's the only one who's ever trusted me that much. But that's exactly why I can't go along with your plan. The need to protect you burns inside me, and if I use you as bait, it'll go against that and every instinct in my body. I can't do it."

Frowning, she shook her head slowly. "But you barely know me, and what about Justin? Isn't he more important? I don't want to be the reason for even worse things to happen than getting his finger cut off."

"He's *not* more important than you, and I know you well enough to know I'll do anything to protect you. We'll find a way to get to Justin back, I promise you that, but it won't be by risking you."

She looked stunned and then she glanced away, looking past him to the window while she took a deep breath. "Like you with your cousin, I've never had anyone besides my uncle who put me or my safety in front of anyone else before," she said softly, her eyes coming back to meet his. "I wish you'd take me back so we can save him, but I promise you that I'll do everything in my power to help you find and rescue him."

"It's a deal, so long as you don't try to put yourself in harms way to do it. Did you call your uncle and let him know what's going on?"

Amusement filled her eyes as she smiled. "Yeah. He wasn't too happy that I was in trouble, and he offered to call his so-called mafia contacts to take care of the Creepy Dudes. He also said to tell you that if you hurt me or anything happens to me, he'll sic those same men on you, and that he has all your info in the hotel's system, so there's no hiding from him."

He chuckled in response, but he was positive her uncle meant every word of that. "The threat isn't needed because I have every intention of taking care of you, but it's duly noted. I'm glad you have someone in your life who cares as he does."

"Me too. I honestly don't know what I would have done without him. Probably stayed dirty and hungry when my mom was still around, and then placed into foster care after she left. He's the best."

Colton couldn't imagine how Katia's mother hadn't loved and taken care of her, but he was glad her uncle stepped in to do those things when her mom dropped the ball. His aunt and uncle might have been distant with him and Justin, but they'd never gone hungry or not been given the things they needed.

"Okay, I need to get a shower. I didn't get a chance this morning, with staying in the truck all night and then getting you the hell out of there. You hungry? I can order a pizza."

"Yeah, that sounds good."

"Don't answer the door for anyone while I'm in the bathroom, okay? I'll be out of the shower fast enough to get the pizza when it gets here."

"I won't."

He studied her gorgeous face for a few more

moments before placing an order for delivery. When he was finished, he grabbed his bag, watching as she settled back onto the bed with her sketchpad.

And the whole time, he was still trying to figure out what in the hell the elusive emotion he felt for her was —but he was no closer to an answer than he'd been the first time he felt it.

Chapter 5

Silence filled the room as Katia's pencil flew over the sketchpad, her eyes quickly moving back and forth between the paper and Colton. The only light in the room came from a dim lamp on the nightstand, but it was enough for her to see him clearly.

When he came out of the bathroom after his shower, it had been all she could do to keep her mouth from popping open. He'd been wearing nothing but a pair of low-slung pajama bottoms, and his glorious, muscular chest was bare.

Her mouth had instantly dried as she took him in, and from that moment on, trying not to stare was one of the hardest things she'd ever done. He somehow looked even larger without his shirt. His pecs were bigger than any she'd seen before, at least in real life, and dusted with light brown hair. The hills and valleys of his abs were well defined, and he had a happy trail that started under his belly button and disappeared beneath his pants, bracketed by a well-defined V that made her wonder if she was drooling.

And she swore his biceps were as big as her thighs.

The moment she saw him walk out of the bathroom in a cloud of steam, she itched to draw him.

She was treated to the mouthwatering view as they ate and then for about an hour afterward as they chatted and watched TV, before he said he was exhausted and laid down. She'd tried so hard to resist the urge to grab her pencils and sketchbook, and she managed it for about an hour before she finally gave in.

Pausing, she gazed at him for a moment, swallowing hard as desire heated her blood and pooled in her belly. He was sprawled out over the bed, so big that he damned near took up the whole surface. One of his arms was behind his head, and the covers had fallen to his waist, giving the illusion that he wasn't wearing anything at all—and he looked sexier than a man had a right to.

She could almost hear the sound of her ovaries exploding as she gazed at him.

Lord, she needed to get herself under control. She was already getting attached to him, and that wasn't good. Their circumstances weren't the least bit normal, but it was getting harder and harder to remember that. She was in so much trouble.

If it was only his looks that she was attracted to, she might stand a chance of keeping herself separate from him. She'd seen good looking men before, after all—although none as gorgeous as Colton. Hell, none of them even came close.

But she was just as attracted to who he was on the inside as she was to his outside. He was kind, caring, protective, and funny. As much as she knew he needed to find his cousin, as worried as he was, he still put her safety first, even when she offered to lure the Bad Guys out.

How could she not think he was even more attractive after getting to know him?

And how the hell was a man like him even still single? Women on the whole were a bunch of idiots, and that'd never been clearer to her than it was after meeting him and finding the absence of a wedding ring on his finger.

Biting her lip, she forced herself to look away and went back to her drawing. He might not be single—just because he didn't wear a wedding ring didn't mean he had no significant other in his life.

Disappointment filled her at the thought that he might have someone at home, so potent it surprised her. Why did she care whether he was single or not? They were only in each other's lives temporarily. As soon as he had Justin back and she was no longer in danger, they'd return to being strangers.

Sadness replaced the disappointment, but she tried to banish it. She might feel like she'd known him forever, but in all reality, she didn't really know him well enough to miss him.

But for whatever reason, she knew she would, just as well as she knew her own name.

Hey, she tried to console herself, *at least you're getting an amazing adventure out of this. It's been the most exciting thing to happen in your boring existence. So, focus on the experience you're having and not the fact that it'll eventually end.*

Her little pep talk did nothing to make her feel better, and she had to snort at herself. She was basically on the run because her life was in danger, and she was calling it an adventure, of all things. And shouldn't she *want* it to end? If it was over, that meant she wouldn't have anyone wanting to kill her because she could identify them.

Maybe her little fantasy that she was in the middle of a romantic movie was becoming too real in her mind. It was better than the terror she'd felt at first, and she felt like she could breathe again after she decided to pretend. But if she was starting to truly believe it, she needed to nip her imagination in the bud and force herself to acknowledge the reality.

Exhaling heavily, she began drawing again, wishing she'd brought her charcoals with her. Or even her paint. She wasn't as good at painting as she was sketching, but she'd like to have this in color. She'd been at it for nearly an hour, taking her time so she could get all the details just right, but she was nearly done. She wanted to remember this moment when she was back in her regular life.

Focusing on the image coming to life in front of her, she lost track of time as she put the finishing details on. She was just closing the book when a knock came on the door. Blinking with surprise, she stilled as she looked over at it, wondering who in the world it could possibly be.

A glance over at Colton showed he was still sleeping, so she shoved her sketchbook into her backpack and stood, padding silently over to the door, taking care not to make any noise.

Easing in close, she looked through the peephole, freezing when she saw two large men outside. Surely Creepy Dudes wouldn't politely knock on the door if they'd found her—right?

They were both wearing ballcaps and sunglasses—the latter of which made her uneasy as hell about their intentions, since it was dark outside—so she couldn't tell if they were the same men. Her sight line was limited, but she didn't see a third man who could be Justin, and she tried to reassure herself that that was good news, and these men had nothing to do with that situation.

But just because he wasn't right there at the door with them didn't mean he wasn't somewhere else, still being held hostage, maybe tied up—or even worse—while the Bad Guys came to take care of their loose end—meaning her.

Biting her lip with indecision, she stared for a few

moments more. They didn't walk away, but she decided if she didn't answer the door, she and Colton were fine. She was just starting to move back when one of them glanced down the hall, and her blood ran cold as she saw the mole on his cheek.

The Bad Guys were definitely there—at least, one of them was. She didn't see a scar on the other one's chin, so this man was different.

And that meant there were more than just two of them involved. That car she saw at the gas station probably *had* been them. They'd figured out she was leaving with Colton and followed them, but they hadn't realized it, because the bastards weren't in the Camry.

Shit on a stick. This wasn't good.

Easing backward, she tiptoed over to the bed, fear and uneasiness coiling together in a knot in her belly and making her queasy. Leaning over Colton, she took a deep breath, pausing as his scent filled her nose.

Damn, he smelled delicious.

It was stupid to stop for even a brief moment to smell him when danger was at their door—literally—but for some odd reason, it calmed her down.

Maybe because it cemented the fact that she wasn't in this alone. She didn't know, but whatever the reason, she was grateful for it. She felt calmer and more in control.

Another soft knock came on the door and her heart knocked painfully against her ribs. Placing her hand on Colton's warm shoulder, she ignored the tingles rushing through her at the contact, shaking him gently at first, and then a little harder.

"Colton," she whispered quietly, afraid the men outside would hear her. "You need to wake up."

His head moved on the pillow as he turned toward her voice, and then his sleepy hazel eyes slowly opened. She immediately put her finger over her mouth, warning him to be quiet. Frowning, he met her eyes, his gaze full of questions.

Leaning in, she put her mouth next to his ear as she whispered. "The Bad Guys are outside the door. Well, one of them is, at least. There are two out there, but only one of them is one I saw before. They're knocking politely for some reason, but they're not going away."

Katia pulled back, watching as his eyes went from sleepy and confused to awake and alert in an instant. He got out of bed with a reassuring smile, but it didn't reach his eyes, and they had a hard glint inside them.

She watched as they became greener with swirls of yellow, narrowing her own when it seemed like his pupil elongated for a moment. He looked away quickly and made his way silently to the door, and she frowned, wondering if that really happened or not.

Every time she saw it, it was in an intense, stressful situation, or they were having an emotional conversation. So, she had to be imagining it. Her mind was playing tricks on her, maybe trying to distract her from the reality of the situation.

Because there was no way it was really happening. It just wasn't possible.

Right?

Colton turned away from the door, his face a thundercloud of emotions. Worry—for her, she thought—mixed with fury, and a poorly masked yearning to open the door and beat answers out of the bastards.

He stalked over to the window and her brow furrowed as he peeked out of the curtain, looking like he was contemplating the window as an exit route. Lord, she hoped not, because they were on the second floor, and she'd surely break her neck.

Walking back over, he grabbed their bags from the floor and set them on the beds. "Get all your stuff ready, just in case," he said, so softly she had to strain to hear him.

Nodding uncertainly, she got her stuff together and slid her shoes on, her mouth drying as she watched him pull a shirt on and then quickly exchange his pajama bottoms for jeans. Sweet baby Jesus, he was so damned hot.

His thighs and legs were just as muscled as the rest of him, and his ass in those boxer briefs... It was taught and round, and she was dying to touch. Swallowing hard as her mouth suddenly flooded with moisture, she forced herself to look away.

She perched on the edge of the bed, watching as he put his shoes on and walked back to the door. He looked out and then turned with a small smile that finally reached his eyes, and the hard knot in her gut slowly unraveled as he walked back over.

"They left."

Her spine slumped with relief for a moment, and she shook her head in bewilderment. "I don't understand why they were knocking. Did they really think we'd just let them in?"

He shrugged as he sat on the opposite bed, facing her with their legs nearly touching. "Maybe they weren't totally sure this was our room, or they thought we wouldn't recognize them with the hats and glasses."

"I don't know how they even found us to begin with. I didn't think anyone saw me leave with you."

"They must have, though, and then they followed us here."

She frowned unhappily. "I honestly wasn't completely convinced they'd even come after me, but I guess this confirms it. I wonder how we're gonna get free of them now that they know I'm with you and what you drive."

He opened his mouth to reply but then he froze, his head jerking toward the door. Standing, he walked toward it, his nose wrinkling as he got closer. Pausing, he looked over at her before he even got there, and she cocked her head as she studied his expression. For the life of her, she couldn't figure out the emotions she found there, but she knew she didn't like them.

"Don't panic, okay? Try to stay calm."

She shot to her feet, dread welling up inside her. "What is it? What's wrong?"

"I smell smoke, and it's getting stronger. We need to get out of here, now."

Colton was crazy if he thought she wasn't going to flip out, and that was exactly what she did. "*What*? Why the hell are we still standing here? We need to get our stuff and get out!"

She snatched up her backpack and slung it on as she grabbed her bag. Starting to walk over to him, she stopped as he held out his hand and shook his head.

"We can't go out of the door. I'd bet everything I own that they started the fire as a way to flush us out and are waiting for us to leave."

Disbelief washed over her as she stared at him incredulously. "And what the hell are we going to do, then? Stay in here and burn to death?"

The fire alarms started going off and she jumped, cursing as the sprinklers in the room came on. It was an idiotic thing to worry about considering the circumstances, but she was going to be so pissed if her sketchbook got ruined.

He walked over next to her and grabbed his bag, raising his voice to be heard over the alarm. "We're not staying in here. We're going out the window."

Mouth popping open, she automatically followed him to the window even as she shook her head vehemently, rejecting his plan. "Are you freakin' crazy? We're on the second floor. We'll both break our necks, so the end result is the same as if we left by the door. Besides, these windows are one solid pane. You can't open them."

"We won't break our necks. I'll jump first and then I'll catch you. As for the window... stand back."

Still shaking her head, she did as he asked, knowing there was no way he could break the window, so it wasn't like they'd be jumping, anyway. Setting his bag down, he picked up a heavy chair, his muscles bulging from the weight, and her jaw dropped as she watched him. She knew he was strong, but how the hell did he manage to pick that up? And so damned effortlessly, like it was a piece of paper and not a solid wooden chair.

A few moments later, he proved she knew nothing about anything as he threw the chair so hard, it shattered both window and chair. Turning around like what he did wasn't a big deal at all, he took her bag and picked his up, tossing them both out of the window.

"I'll go first. Once I'm down and ready, follow me, okay?"

Moving forward, she risked a glance out of the window, swallowing hard at the distance to the ground. "I don't think I can do that."

"Hey," he said softly, moving in close and framing her face with his hands. "I promise I'll catch you. I'll never let anything happen to you, Katia."

She felt like everything inside her stilled at his touch, and she searched his eyes, finding nothing but promise and resolve. Somehow, she found herself nodding in agreement even as she cursed inside, asking herself what the hell she thought she was doing.

Colton winked at her, stealing her breath, and turned, knocking the glass off the bottom of the window frame. Without pausing, he jumped out, and she rushed to the window just as he landed. How in the ever-loving hell did he land so gracefully? He made it look like it was nothing at all to jump from a two-story window and land easily on his feet.

He turned and beckoned to her, but she couldn't make herself move. The smell of smoke was a lot stronger now, and she thought she could even hear the crackling of the fire, but still, she couldn't get up the courage.

"Come on," Colton called from below. Turning back to the window, she saw him beckoning to her. "I promise I'll catch you. You can do this, sweetheart."

Despite the terror she felt at the thought of jumping, and the urgency washing over her as the fire neared, she still swooned a little inside when he called her sweetheart. And of all the things he'd said, it was weirdly the one word that motivated her to swing her legs over the windowsill.

It let her know he actually believed she could do this, and it made her think he cared enough that he wouldn't let her die.

Nerves welled up inside her as she stared at the distance between herself and the ground, so she closed her eyes as she took a deep breath. Not letting herself think about it anymore, she pushed herself off the ledge as the wind flew past her and the ground rushed up to meet her.

COLTON

Please God let him catch me.

COLTON WATCHED KATIA AS HE HELPED HER INTO THE truck. Her black curls were in disarray around her face, and her sky-blue eyes were still wide and shell shocked. She hadn't said anything except *thank God* since he caught her, and he felt worry well up inside him as he shut the door and walked to his side.

He couldn't blame her for being freaked out, though. He thought he would be too, if he was a human. Hell, he *had* been freaked out, worried she'd slip through his grip or he wouldn't catch her.

Being a shifter, he'd known he could easily jump out of the window and land with no problems, and he'd been confident that he could catch her—mostly. Doubt had tried to creep in, and he thought it was because he couldn't handle the thought of her getting hurt.

He was already more attached to her than he'd ever imagined he would be, especially this soon. But there was no denying that he was, for good or for bad. It was why the thought of taking her back to Atlanta and using her as bait had made him feel simultaneously violent and ill.

Jumping out of the window had been a risk he hated, but it was a necessary one. His gut said the bastards who had Justin started the fire, and they were waiting for them to come out of their room—by way of the door.

Even now, he hated the fact that they had to be out in the open briefly to get away, and he cringed as he started the truck and it came to life with a loud growl. Quickly putting it in gear, he pulled out as fast as he could without attracting attention, the flashing lights of the firetrucks and police cars lighting up the road behind them.

Using it to make sure no one was following them, he got on the ramp for the interstate, thankful the hotel was close to it. Once they were on the way, he glanced over at Katia, wishing he could read her mind and tell whether she was okay.

"You doing okay over there?"

She glanced over at him and his eyebrows rose as he saw the slight smile on her face. "Yeah. It was scary as hell, but that was the most exhilarating experience of my life. I actually ended up enjoying it."

Relief washed over him, and he felt his lips curl up in a smile at the shock and enthusiasm in her voice. "It was a rush, right?"

"It definitely was." Biting her lip, she went quiet for a moment. "So what now? They know who both of us are and what we're driving. I'm even more for going back to Atlanta now and drawing them out so we can end this before one or both of us gets hurt."

Exhaling, he tightened his hands on the steering wheel as he shook his head. "I still don't think that's a good idea."

It's definitely not a good idea, his dragon hissed, not liking that plan any more than he did.

I know. I don't know what to do next, though. I can't look for Justin and keep her fully protected at the same time. It's clear that they want to silence her for being able to identify them.

His dragon went quiet inside him, and when he spoke again, his voice was dripping with reluctance. *Maybe she has a point.*

What? About going back to Atlanta? She'd be in danger, he retorted, scowling. He couldn't believe his animal would even suggest it.

Like she's not now? At least this way, we can get Justin away from the bastards and make sure she stays *safe. We can end this.*

Fuck. Why was he even starting to *think* his dragon had a point?

"I *do* think it's a good idea," Katia replied, bringing him back to the conversation. "And we don't have to do this alone. My uncle knows what's going on. He can help. I might not believe he or any of my family are in the mob, but he has some terrifying, badass friends, there's no denying that."

Cocking an eyebrow, he glanced over at her. "He let you be around terrifying men?"

She waved her hand dismissively. "They were never anything but nice to me. I wouldn't want to be a stranger and meet them in a dark alley, though."

He shook his head as he checked the rearview mirror, relieved that the road was as dark and empty as it had been when they first got on the interstate. "You have an interesting life."

Her eyebrows rose and she laughed as she looked at him. "No, not at all. My life is beyond boring. I just know some interesting people, is all."

Exhaling, he considered her words about her uncle, but he honestly didn't know what the hell to do. He wasn't used to not knowing exactly what to do next, and he hated it. The indecision literally grated on his nerves.

The thought of having help eased some of his fear for Katia's safety, but he still had no clue who the bastards after her were. Or rather, *what* they were. If they were humans, her uncle's friends would come in handy. If they were shifters... everyone could end up dead at the end of it.

No, they won't, his dragon said resolutely inside him. *Remember, you have me, and we're almost indestructible in my form. We won't let anyone die and we'll kill those fuckers for daring to mess with Katia and Justin.*

Did you forget that we have to hide what we are? If I have to shift—and in the middle of Atlanta, of all places—it not only lets humans know shifters exist, but it puts a big target on our backs. Humans and hunters alike will be hunting us and trying to kill us.

Would that stop you from shifting to defend Katia or Justin? his dragon asked quietly.

He didn't answer because there was no point in it. He and his dragon both knew he wouldn't hesitate. If it came down to a choice between saving them and exposing what he was, or keeping the secret and letting them die, he'd choose them in a heartbeat.

"I've been watching, and we weren't followed this time. Let's get another room for the night and we can decide then what we'll do tomorrow."

A glance over at her showed her narrowing her eyes on him, and he knew she didn't believe he'd give in about going back. It was the last thing he wanted to do, but dammit all, he was actually contemplating it. It was a risk, but if it meant keeping her safe and getting Justin back, it would be worth it.

If he could do those things.

"Okay. But don't think I'm just gonna give up on trying to convince you to go back."

His lips curled as he huffed a laugh. "I never imagined for a moment that you would."

"What do you do for a living? I don't think you ever mentioned it," she said after a short silence.

"I have a small ranch in Montana. Actually, it's mine and Justin's. His parents left it to us about seven years ago when they moved to Maine."

"They left it to both of you?" she asked, surprise in her voice.

He shrugged, slowing down to take the next exit off the interstate. "Yeah. My parents died when I was five and I went to live with them. They said I'd become as much their son as Justin, and they know we're close, so they left it to both of us."

She was quiet for a moment before speaking again. "I'm so sorry about your parents."

"It's okay. I missed them something fierce at first,

but it was twenty-five years ago. I hardly remember them now."

"Still, it sucks. So, you and Justin are probably closer than just cousins, then, if you literally grew up together."

"Yeah. We're more like brothers, and he's my best friend."

"All the more reason to go with my plan."

Shaking his head, he didn't reply as he parked at the new hotel. He was so torn about what their next move should be. Yeah, going back to Atlanta would get him Justin back and finally end this.

But she could get hurt, and he'd rather die himself than lose her.

Dramatic, maybe, but it was precisely how he felt. And it just confirmed what he already suspected.

He was falling for her hard, and there was no slowing it down or stopping it. He didn't even want to.

Chapter 6

Katia glanced over, taking in the grim set to Colton's mouth. She couldn't see his eyes since they were fixed on the road, but she was sure the hazel depths were just as worried as they'd been when they left the hotel.

He'd been extremely reluctant, but he finally gave in and agreed to her plan, so they were back on the road to Atlanta. She couldn't deny that she was pretty scared to go back and willingly put herself in the Bad Guys sights again, but she also knew it was the best option they had, to both end this and for Colton to get his cousin back.

She snuck a glance over at him and her heart immediately jumped in response. It was clear as day to her that she was falling for him—but she couldn't help wondering if it was real or just a product of the fantasy she'd had in the beginning.

Really, she hadn't thought of that romantic movie scenario since the beginning, but still, it made her wonder. He'd become the hero in that moment, so were the feelings she was developing strictly because of that?

Honestly, she didn't think so. They felt as real and tangible as anything in her life ever had, but that made her nervous, too. Because even if he felt things for her too, where did that leave them? They lived in completely different parts of her country, her in Georgia and him in Montana, and they'd both created lives for themselves.

Granted, hers wasn't much of one, but she still had her schooling to think about. She'd worked too long and too hard to throw it all away.

She rolled her eyes at her thoughts, exasperated with herself. She didn't even know if he had feelings for her at all yet, and even if he did, what made her think he'd want to continue seeing her once this was all over?

And that thought made her feel sad as hell.

Lord, her emotions were all over the place today.

"Remember," Colton rumbled, his deep voice filling the truck cab and sending a shiver of heat down her spine. "You stay in my eyesight at all times. I appreciate your uncle's friends being willing to help catch the bastards, but I still don't trust anyone else when it comes to your safety."

Her heart warmed and she couldn't keep a smile from spreading across her face. Other than her uncle, she never had anyone in her life who cared enough to be that concerned for her safety. Maybe it didn't really mean anything, but it made her feel special, like she was someone important—at least to someone.

"I promise."

Giving her a half-smile, he reached over and squeezed her hand before putting it back on the steering wheel. Her belly filled with butterflies as heat licked up her spine, just from that simple touch. Swallowing hard, she blew out a quiet breath, trying to get ahold of her emotions.

She shouldn't feel so much just from the touch of his hand on hers—it was insane to, right? But that, at least, had been real and in no way her imagination, and it reassured her just a little that she wasn't making up the attraction that arched between them.

Her blood was humming in her veins as she watched his big hands lightly gripping the wheel, and she pulled out her sketchbook, deciding she wanted to draw them. She'd always loved men's hands, and his were perfect to her—big and strong, with veins on the front, slightly calloused on the palms.

She couldn't capture the way they made her feel in a sketch, but she could capture the way they looked. On rainy days, once this was over, she could pull out her sketches of him and remember the adventure she went on and the crazy strong attraction she felt for him.

Sadness washed over her at the thought of it ending, and she pushed it away, burying it deep as she concentrated. When she finally looked up, the sketch was done and Colton was taking the exit her hotel was located off of.

Nerves and fear welled up inside her, but she tried not to let it show as she put her things away. Coming back here had been her idea, after all, and she still thought it was a good one. And she didn't want to do anything that gave him second thoughts or made him take her away again.

He was reluctant enough as it was. No need to add to it.

When they pulled up at the hotel, the first thing she saw was her uncle, standing by the entrance with four of his friends. They were all standing with their arms crossed and dark scowls on their faces, and they looked menacing enough that they were going to scare all potential customers away.

But she loved the fact that none of them, Sergei especially, looked like they gave a shit if the hotel lost business.

The moment the truck was in park, she opened her door, not waiting for Colton to come around to help her out. Her uncle immediately made his way toward her, and she'd just put her backpack on when he pulled her into a tight bear hug.

"Can't. Breathe," she wheezed out, laughing in between inhalations of air when he eased away, putting his hands on her shoulders.

"You okay, girlie?"

Some of the nerves and fear seeped away as she heard the nickname he gave her years ago, spoken in his gruff Russian accent. Smiling as she kissed his cheek, she tried to make sure the remaining fear was buried deeply enough that he couldn't see it in her eyes.

"I'm fine, Sergei. I haven't been hurt, and I'm just ready to end this now."

He smiled back, approval shining from his blue eyes. "That's my brave girl. Show those murderous bastards that you can't be intimidated or silenced."

Colton walked around the front of the trucks with their bags in his hands and her uncle turned toward him. His friends greeted her warmly, and then they joined her uncle in gazing at Colton with narrowed, critical eyes.

"You the man who thinks he can protect my girl?" Sergei said, his eyes not the least bit friendly.

Putting the bags down, Colton offered him his hand. "I'm Colt, sir, and it's good to meet you, although I wish it was under different circumstances—and I don't *think* I can protect her. I *know* I can."

Sergei didn't immediately shake his hand, and Katia held her breath as he drew the moment out. After what felt like an eternity, Colton's hand and the steady eye contact with him never wavering, her uncle finally huffed a breath as he shook it.

"You better, boy, or you're the one whose life is

going to be in danger. You're the one who got her into this mess."

She shook her head with a roll of her eyes. "Now Sergei, you know that isn't true."

"Well, it's close enough. Him, his family, it's all the same."

Opening her mouth, she started to protest but Colton spoke before she could. "You're right, it does fall on my family's shoulders. You have my word that I won't let anything happen to her. I won't let it."

Sergei studied him closely and then finally nodded, glancing back at her. "Well, let's all get inside. No need to be out in the open and make her a sitting duck."

Colton picked up the bags and walked with her uncle's friends. She started to follow, but Sergei held her back for a moment before strolling with her after them.

"You like him, don't you? He likes you, too. I can see it in your eyes, especially when you look at each other."

She hesitated, watching Colton's big form as he walked to the hotel door, somehow managing to juggle the bags and hold the door open for Sergei's friends at the same time. He glanced back at her, waiting for her to catch up, and she knew it was because he didn't want her out of his sight—even when she was with her uncle.

"Yeah, I like him, but I don't know if the feeling's mutual."

"Trust me, it definitely is." He ran his eyes over

Colton, lingering on his cowboy hat and boots. "A cowboy, huh? You couldn't have found yourself a nice Russian boy?"

She laughed, but she didn't feel very much humor over the situation. "It won't go that far, Sergei. It can't."

Frowning, he looked over at her, and she knew he wanted to say more. But they thankfully caught up with Colton, effectively keeping her uncle from saying anything else on the subject.

For now, anyway.

She led Colton to her room, knowing he wasn't going to let her stay in there by herself. Her heart fluttered at the thought of the single king bed, but logically she knew he'd probably take the couch.

Didn't stop her from imagining what might happen if he did, though.

Opening the door, she held it for him then followed him in, setting her backpack on her bed and watching as he looked around. She'd made the room as much her own as she could, but it was still clearly a hotel room.

For a split second, she felt embarrassed that he was seeing for himself where she lived. What twenty-six-year-old lived in a hotel instead of having her own place? But she quickly brushed it away.

She worked hard for what she had, and she was damned proud of what she was doing with her life. She'd never felt ashamed of what she had to do to pay for school and still survive, and she wasn't going to let herself start now.

"Should I go ahead and get to work at the front desk? Give them the chance to know I'm here."

He frowned as he shook his head, and she narrowed her gaze. His eyes went that strange kaleidoscope green and yellow and his pupils flickered again, elongating briefly before returning to normal, and this time she knew she wasn't seeing things.

It really happened—which meant Colton was something more than human. He had to be, for his eyes to do that.

Katia thought that should maybe make her nervous or scared of him, but it didn't. Instead, she felt fascinated and curiosity burned through her. What could he possibly be?

And was she truly a few fries short of a Happy Meal? Because she wasn't as scared as she should be that her life was in danger, and now she was positive Colton was more than human and she was curious instead of freaking out.

"No," he replied, bringing her back to the conversation. "I think you can wait until tomorrow. Besides, we were outside long enough that if they were watching right now, they already know you're back."

She searched his eyes, seeing the reluctance he was trying to hide. "It really bothers you that I didn't go inside as soon as we got here, doesn't it? And you do realize you'll have to let me go back to work eventually, right? Otherwise, coming back here was completely pointless."

He exhaled heavily, adjusting his cowboy hat. "I

know. I just… well, I fucking hate the idea of you deliberately putting yourself out there to get them to try to kill you. I'm going to protect you, no matter what I have to do, but I still can't stand the thought of you in danger."

Breath catching, she felt her heart melting and she walked over to him, gently cupping his cheek. She hadn't meant to do that, but she didn't regret it at all. His beard scratched her palm as he leaned into her touch, briefly closing his eyes, and desire and affection shot straight through her veins.

"I understand what you're saying," she replied, clearing her throat when her voice came out all breathy. "I'd feel the same way if the situation was reversed. But I totally trust you to keep me safe, and this is the best way to get Justin back. I know how much you need that, and I'm pretty sure they wouldn't have stopped chasing us anyway. At least this way, we're on my home turf, and we have backup."

Uncertainty flashed through his hazel eyes, followed by something she couldn't identify. "I think you're right. I just hate the situation, all the way around. I'm not going to be able to relax until you're safe and Justin's back."

"I completely understand that," she replied softly, trailing her fingers down his cheek as she pulled her hand away.

He reached up, capturing her hand and holding it against his chest. Her breath caught as he searched her eyes, his gaze soft and affectionate—and slowly filling with heat. She could feel his heart pounding beneath her palm, and hers reacted, beating in tandem with his.

Her breathing stalled completely as he slowly leaned down, and the last thing she saw before her eyes fluttered closed was his pupils flickering again. His lips gently touched hers, his beard lightly scratching her skin, and a wave of heat instantly washed over her as fire sizzled in her veins.

He kissed her softly at first, slowly deepening it, and she moaned as desire forcefully washed over her. Moving in closer, she went up on tiptoe, wrapping her rams around his neck. Her movements knocked his cowboy hat off and she used the opportunity to gently rake her fingernails over his scalp.

Colton groaned deep in his chest, the sound vibrating through her as he grasped her hips and pulled her in tightly against him. The groan tapered off into a strange hissing sound, but instead of freaking her out like she thought it should, it just amped her up even more.

One of his hands gripped her hip tightly and he trailed the other slowly up until he was cupping her face, angling his head as he opened his mouth. She followed suit, and then it was all long, open mouth kisses until he ran his tongue across her lips.

She gasped as her body reacted, lava rushing through her veins as it felt like her whole body tingled, and he used the chance to slip his tongue inside. She met it with her own, pressing her body even more tightly against his, her heart jumping in her chest as she felt his erection digging into her.

His hand tunneled through her curls, gripping tightly as his other moved around to her ass. Their tongues dueled for long moments and then he pulled back and nipped her bottom lip hard before sucking it into his mouth. She moaned, doing her best to get even closer to him, but they were already pressed so tightly together that the only way she was going to get closer was to crawl inside his skin.

He slid his tongue back into her mouth, and she was considering tearing his clothes off then and there when a knock came at the door, followed by her uncle's voice. She jumped, automatically trying to pull away, but Colton didn't let her. He gentled the kiss, slowly easing them down, and then gently nipped her bottom lip one more time before he pulled away.

They were both breathing heavily, and she forced her eyes open, looking up at him. His eyes were full kaleidoscope, the colors bright, and his pupils were elongated. He winked at her and bent to pick up his cowboy hat, settling it on his head as he turned away, hooking his hands on his hips. He was still fighting for breath just as she was, and she hadn't missed the truly impressive bulge of his erection in his jeans.

Yeah, he probably didn't want her uncle to see that, and neither did she.

Blowing out a breath, she fought to even out her breathing, running a hand through her curls. A glance in the mirror showed that they were in complete disarray, her cheeks were pink, and her lips were swollen from that truly amazing kiss.

Sergei knocked again and she blew out a breath as she went to open the door. It was clear to her that she totally looked like she'd just been practically ravished, but she was hoping he wouldn't notice.

A hope that was blown all to hell the moment she opened the door and his eyebrows shot up. A knowing grin spread across his face as he looked from her to Colton, who still had his back turned to them.

"I just wanted to invite you two to dinner in my suite tonight. At six. Show up or not, it's up to you. I don't want to get in the way of any plans you might have."

He winked at her and turned to stride away, leaving her sputtering after him. Amusement filled her as she finally closed the door and turned back around. Colton was staring at her with a wry smile, and as she moved closer, she noticed his eyes had nearly returned to normal.

Was he half snake or lizard or something? What else could account for his eyes and the hiss she heard as they kissed?

Not knowing was driving her crazy, and she was determined to ask him about it later.

"I guess it's pretty obvious what we were up to. You look well kissed right now."

Katia grinned at the satisfaction in his voice. "Well, that's because I was. It was a hell of a kiss."

He nodded, starting to take a step forward and then

pausing with a shake of his head. "If I touch you right now, I won't be able to stop, and we have a dinner to get to. But yes, it was one hell of an amazing kiss."

Her heart warmed, spreading the amazing heat throughout her body. It was different than the heat she felt from the kiss. It wasn't desire, it was the feeling of being cared about—something she'd felt from Colton from nearly the moment they met.

It was amazing, and everything she never thought she'd have, and she was almost certain it was real. There was still a niggling doubt in the back of her mind that had her questioning if this was real or a part of her fantasy, but she was accepting more and more that it was real.

Now the question was, what was she going to do about it?

Colton walked with Katia back to her room, his mind on the dinner they just had. Her uncle and his friends were an interesting group of men, that was sure. She thought Sergei's claims of the Russian mafia were just stories, but he wasn't so sure. He'd seen the look in their eyes throughout dinner, and just that made him inclined to believe the stories were real.

Every time they looked at him, the warning had been clear. Mess with Katia and they'd fuck him up—if not kill him outright.

He slanted a look over at her. Her black curls swayed as she walked, and she was wearing a figure-hugging tank top and snug jeans. Her makeup was minimal and she had old flip flops on her feet, and he thought even as dressed down as she was that she was the most beautiful woman he'd ever seen.

And the woman she was on the inside was even more beautiful. She had a big heart and she genuinely cared about the people around her. She even cared about Justin, and she'd never met him. Some of it had to do with her knowing how important he was to Colton, but he knew she would have cared regardless. That was just the kind of person she was. She was kind, smart, funny, and insanely talented.

He'd hurt himself a million times over before he ever hurt her. Sergei and his friends had nothing to worry about there.

Colton was already a goner when it came to her, and when this was all over and he had Justin back, he wasn't sure if he'd be able to leave her.

His dragon hissed in a breath, shock rolling off him in waves. *Of course. I can't believe I didn't see it before now. I was just so consumed with keeping her safe and saving Justin...*

Colton frowned, knowing his animal wasn't talking about an immediate threat but unable to keep his eyes from darting around, trying to find one. *What didn't you see?*

She... well, Katia's our mate.

He sucked in a breath as the entire universe seemed to stall. *She's our mate? You're sure about that?*

Positive. I knew how you felt for her was unusual for

you, but I was so focused on other stuff that I didn't see why you were getting attached so fast. There's no doubt in my mind, though. She's our mate.

Shock filled him as he swallowed hard. Now that he thought about it, it should have been obvious what she was to him. He'd felt so much for her from the very start and gotten attached so fast.

It explained why even though it tore him up to not go after Justin, the need to get her to safety overpowered it. He liked to think he'd do the same for anyone inadvertently caught in the middle, but he literally burned with the need to keep her safe, and he had from the very start.

Shit. He had a *mate* now.

And how in the hell had he gotten lucky enough for it to be Katia?

"Colt? Are you okay?"

Her voice pulled him back to the present and he blinked with surprise when he realized they were already at her door. She'd opened it and walked inside, holding it for him, and he'd been lost in the shock and wonder of learning she was his mate.

And as he stood there, he couldn't deny the pure joy at the thought of this beautiful woman as his mate.

Clearing his throat, he nodded as he walked inside. "Yeah, I'm fine. Just realizing something."

"Realizing what?"

She let the door close as she asked the question, but he didn't reply. Grabbing her hand, he pulled her into him and kissed her, pouring all the emotions he felt into it.

When he let her go, her gorgeous sky-blue eyes were dazed, and her chest was heaving as she sucked air in. He couldn't keep his eyes from dropping as he watched the movement, but he finally managed to pull them away, looking up and meeting her gaze.

"What was that for?" she whispered, touching her glistening lips with her fingers.

"I just wanted to kiss you."

"Oh. Good reason."

Chuckling, he watched as she walked to the bed and sank down on the edge, her gaze speculative as it rested on him. He arched an eyebrow as he sat on the chair facing her, waiting on her to say what was on her mind.

"Will you tell me the truth if I ask you something?"

His brow furrowed as he cocked his head. "Of course."

"Why do your eyes change? They go from hazel to this kaleidoscope of green and yellow, and your pupils elongate. I think it's clear that you're not quite human, but what exactly are you?"

Freezing, he stared at her in surprise. He hadn't once given thought to how his eyes changed when he was riled up emotionally and his dragon was close to the surface. That was probably stupid, to never consider it or try to hide it, but it never crossed his mind with her.

Nerves welled up inside him and he rolled his

shoulders, uncomfortable with the feeling. It wasn't an emotion he ever felt, and he had a hard time processing it.

Calm down, his dragon rumbled inside him, his voice smooth and unruffled. *She obviously noticed it a while ago, and her question was curious, not freaked out. Not to mention that she wouldn't have let you kiss her if it bothered her.*

Okay, his animal had a point. Inhaling deeply, he forced the nerves down deep and met her curious gaze. "No, I'm not quite human. I'm a shifter."

Her eyes went wide as her eyebrows shot up. "A shifter?"

"Yeah. I share my body with an animal, and I shift into that form sometimes. We're the same yet separate —it's hard to explain. He has his own thoughts and emotions, but we're still one."

"Wow," she breathed, fascination in her light blue eyes. "What kind of animal do you have? Your pupils make me think something like a snake, but I can't see that fitting the man I know you are, at all."

Searching her eyes, he hesitated as he tried to decide if he should ease her into it or just blurt it out. He'd never told anyone what kind of animal he was before. All dragons kept that information close to their chests, not wanting to be targets of hunters.

He wasn't at all worried about that from Katia, of course, and it wasn't that he didn't *want* to tell her. He just didn't know how she'd react to it. She was handling the fact that he was a shifter well but admitting that he was a dragon might be what sent her running.

Maybe the best way to do it was to just rip it off like a Band-Aid. Quick and painless.

Hopefully.

"I'm not a snake. I'm a dragon."

He hadn't thought her eyes could get any wider, but they did as her breathing stalled. Swallowing hard, she huffed out a breath as she slowly shook her head. He didn't think it was in denial, but rather in shock as she tried to process it.

The silence stretched out, and the nerves were starting to well up again when she finally spoke.

"A dragon? Seriously? That's so cool."

Blinking at the enthusiasm in her voice, he smiled slowly as relief filled him. "You really think so, don't you?"

"Hell yes! Do you look like dragons in movies? Scaly, horned, big as a house? What color are you?"

He chuckled at the barrage of questions. "Yeah, the movies actually give pretty accurate depictions of us. I'm green with a yellow underbelly."

"I'd love to see him some day. Do you have anything you can do differently than the rest of us?"

"I'd love to show him to you some day," he replied, awe for her overwhelming him for a moment. She was a hell of woman, there was no doubting that—not that he ever had. "We're stronger and faster, and we don't get sick. We heal very fast, and things that can kill a human are less likely to kill us. We have excellent vision and hearing. And every shifter has a gift, something different and special."

"Really? What's yours?"

"Yeah, some are physical, some are mental, and they can be a human trait that's enhanced or something totally supernatural. Mine's controlling the elements."

"Like weather and stuff?"

"That's part of it." Pausing, he concentrated hard, chuckling as she jumped at the loud clap of thunder he produced.

"That was you?"

"Yeah." Holding out his hand, he focused on it, watching as a ball of fire appeared, hovering over his palm. "It's mostly that I can control earth, air, water, and fire, like this."

Getting up, she moved closer, studying the fire in his palm. "That doesn't burn you?"

"No, but it'll hurt others just like real fire. It doesn't affect me because I created it. If I were to create a tornado, I could stand in the middle and not even feel a breeze from it."

"That's amazing. I can't imagine being able to do something like that."

Letting the fire die away, he shrugged as she moved to sit back down. "When it first started developing, I thought it was the coolest thing in the world, and I played with my abilities constantly. I guess as I got older, it became commonplace, just something I could do. Not all shifter gifts are as powerful as that, though.

Some are pretty normal. Like Justin's. His is the ability to go without sleep."

She smiled ruefully. "That seems pretty amazing to me. Working two jobs and going to school means I don't have as much time to study as I'd like. And that also means I have no life, because most of my spare time is spent studying."

"You're pretty amazing, you know that, right?"

"What? Why?"

"Because you have a dream and you're not afraid to work for it. You even turned down a full ride because you wanted to do it yourself. You convinced me to bring you back here, where you're in danger, just to help my cousin. And I just told you something that most would either not believe and they'd think I'm nuts, or they'd run screaming away from me as fast as they could go. And yet here you sit, calmly asking me questions about it. You're sweet, kind, smart, talented, and you have a big heart. I can't believe you don't see for yourself just how amazing you are."

Her cheeks pinkened with a blush as she glanced down at her hands. "I'm just doing what anyone else would do."

He shook his head as she glanced back up, meeting his gaze. "No. You're not. Trust me on that."

"Well, whether I am or not, thank you for those words. I'm not really going after my dream, though. That's art. I'm just going after an occupation that gives me a good chance of using my dream in some small way."

"Either way, you're doing everything you can to achieve your goal, so my words still stand."

She smiled, ducking her head, and his heart felt so full as he gazed at her. He was still in awe that she was his mate, and he didn't think the feeling would fade any time soon. He'd imagined what his mate would be like over the years, if he was lucky enough to find her, but he couldn't have dreamed up a woman as gorgeous and amazing as Katia.

His imagination just wasn't good enough for that.

Neither was mine, his dragon whispered inside him. *She's so much more than I expected.*

He and his animal had always been in accord, but never more than in that moment, as he watched the woman he was falling for.

Did he maybe even love her already? He'd never been in love before, so he couldn't be sure. But his gut said if he wasn't fully there yet, he was very close. And it didn't bother him at all.

He couldn't imagine anything better than loving her—unless it was her loving him back.

Chapter 7

Katia brushed her still damp hair back from her face, biting her lip as she concentrated on her newest sketch. Colton was taking his turn in the shower, and she was hoping to get this finished before he got out.

Pausing, she studied the image, wondering how close she'd gotten it. To one side was Colton, standing with his arms crossed, cowboy hat perched on his head and a grin on his face. On the other, she was drawing his dragon—or at least what he looked like in her head.

It was still a little mind blowing that he was a shifter, and his animal was a dragon, of all things. But it fascinated her. She thought if anyone else had told her that, she wouldn't have believed them in a million years, or if she had, she would have been scared out of her mind.

But she immediately believed him, and she hadn't been a bit scared of him after learning what he was. It was a little ironic, though. The mafia was a group that very definitely existed and was real, but she never believed her uncle when he told her stories. Yet Colton told her that he was a supernatural being who shared his body with a *dragon*, and she never once questioned it.

Maybe it was because she'd seen his eyes change for herself. She'd known before he told her that there was something different about him. After all, normal humans didn't have pupils that elongated.

It probably went a long way in making her so certain he was telling the truth, but she thought even if she hadn't seen it, she still might believe him. She knew in her bones that he was an honest man, and he wouldn't lie to her about something like that.

If she'd had any doubts, though, seeing his gift would have wiped them clean. Man, what a gift! Controlling the elements would be amazing. Pausing in the middle of finishing off one of the dragon's horns, she quickly sketched a tornado behind Colton, nodding when she saw it all together.

She was just finishing the horn when she heard the shower shut off. Gazing at the image one more time, satisfaction filled her and she smiled as she closed the sketchbook and put it on the bedside table.

A few moments later, he walked out of the bathroom, and she swallowed hard as she adjusted the glasses she was wearing. He was once again in just a pair of low riding pajama bottoms, and his skin was still a little damp.

How was it possible that a man could be as good looking at him? She hadn't thought it could be, outside of the movies and magazines.

He glanced at her, eyebrows raising and a slow smile curling his lips up. "I didn't know you wore glasses."

Reaching up, she touched the black frames self-consciously. "Only at night when my eyes are tired, and I want to focus on something."

"They're sexy as fuck on you, Katia," he replied, his voice husky and deep.

Her self-consciousness faded as heat filled her cheeks. What was with her blushing so much? She didn't usually do it often, but she'd done it a lot since meeting him. "Thank you."

Eyes full of warmth, he winked at her, and then his gaze dropped, slowly sliding over the tank top and shorts she always slept in. When he met her gaze again, his eyes were swirling with green and yellow, and so full of heat, they nearly singed her where she sat.

Looking away, he cleared his throat, a muscle in his jaw flexing. After inhaling deeply, he looked back over at her. "Where can I go get an extra blanket for the couch?"

"Shoot," she said, uncurling her legs and standing up. "I'll go get it. It totally slipped my mind."

While she was walking past him, he snagged her hand, pulling her up against him. She gasped as she came in contact with his hot skin, and her hands immediately went to his chest. She'd just meant to steady herself, but she couldn't help sliding her hands over the muscular planes, swooning inside at the feel of his skin, and the heat and desire that washed over her.

"I think I need a kiss before you go anywhere."

A shiver of heat danced up her spine as she felt the rumble of his words underneath her palms. "I think you do too," she whispered in agreement.

"As sexy as these are, I think they'll just get in the way," he said, gently plucking her glasses off and sitting them on the dresser next to them.

Leaning in, he kissed her gently and then slowly deepened it, just as he had for their first kiss. She thought she knew what to expect, that she knew how she was going to feel, but it was even more intense than it was before.

A wave of desire nearly knocked her over, and she leaned into him more fully, needing the support as her knees weakened. He ran his tongue over her lips and she opened for him, meeting it with hers as her core tightened in response.

What this man did to her was unbelievable. Fire was burning through her veins, and she felt like she was going to spontaneously combust at any moment.

His hands dropped to her ass and he pulled her in closer, his fingers kneading the globes and making the desire she felt nearly unbearable.

Arching her back, she pressed against his rapidly forming erection. He made a hissing growl noise, and maybe she was weird, but knowing it was because he was feeling something strong enough that it made his dragon come close to the surface only turned her on more.

Easing back, he nipped at her bottom lip, harder than he had before, and then soothed the spot with his tongue. "Keep that up and I won't be able to let you go anywhere."

"And maybe I don't need to," she replied breathlessly as she met his kaleidoscope green eyes. "I'm thinking that bed is definitely big enough for the both of us."

The desire in his gaze flared hotter and he immediately walked her backward to the king bed, not stopping until the backs of her knees touched the mattress. "You'll get no argument from me on that one, sweetheart."

A smile slowly spread across her face and she pushed him a few steps back. Confusion filled his gaze but before he could say anything, she climbed on the bed. Once she was settled, she crooked her finger at him.

"What are you waiting for?"

Sucking in a breath, he ran his gaze over her slowly, and she swore she felt it like he was physically touching her. Meeting her gaze, he climbed onto the bed and crawled toward her, keeping eye contact with her the whole time. Her core clenched tightly again as desire and butterflies mixed together in her belly.

She eased down on the pillows as he crawled over her, resting his weight on his elbows as he framed her face with his hands. Immediately pressing his lips to hers, he kissed her deeply as he eased his body onto hers. She gasped as she felt his body come into contact fully with hers, arching her back to press against him tighter.

Easing out of the kiss, he slid his mouth across her cheek to her ear and then licked and nipped his way down her neck. Rolling her head to the side, she gave him better access, moaning as he lightly bit down on the tendon of her neck and shoulder.

His other hand trailed down her side, his thumb lightly brushing the side of her breast, and then he paused on her hip before making his way back up. This time, he cupped it fully, his hand big enough that he nearly covered the whole globe.

He groaned deep in his chest as he kneaded it, his words muffled against her neck. "I knew you weren't wearing a bra. Fuck, Katia."

She smiled with satisfaction at the clearly strained tone in his voice, but the next moment, she let out a groan of her own as he rubbed his thumb over her nipple. He pressed kisses to her skin, slowly making his way across her chest, sliding his tongue across the skin above her tank top.

Easing back, he pulled it down until it was caught underneath her breasts, his breath stalling as he gazed at her. "You're so fucking gorgeous."

Before she had a chance to reply, he leaned down and flicked her nipple with his tongue before sucking it into his mouth. Gasping, she shut her eyes tightly as sensations exploded inside her. It felt like there was a direct line from her nipple to her clit, and every pull of his mouth set off fireworks inside her.

Shifting his weight, he trailed his hand down her stomach, slipping it inside her shorts as his mouth switched to her other nipple. Anticipation flooded her veins as he paused for a never-ending moment, and she was just about to demand he move when he finally did, cupping her mound.

She'd tried to prepare herself for how it'd feel when his fingers slipped inside and rubbed her swollen nub, but she never could have prepared for that. A strong wave of pleasure washed over her, and she was glad she was lying down, because it would have knocked her on her ass if she'd been standing.

His fingers circled her clit and then he dipped a finger inside her, pulling it out and adding a second. Her back arched off the bed as he pumped them slowly in and out, and then he returned to her clit, flicking it just as he lightly bit her nipple.

She cried out, unable to help herself, and his fingers moved faster and harder, until he finally rubbed directly over her nub. Pleasure burst over her and she exploded, flying apart as her body shuddered in an orgasm more intense than she'd ever felt.

When she finally floated back to the ground, Colton was kissing his way up her heaving chest, then sliding his mouth up her neck, his beard lightly tickling her skin. He pressed a light kiss to her lips and she sighed, her body shuddering one more time.

"Colt..."

"Yes, love?" he murmured, nuzzling her neck.

Her heart warmed at his endearment at the same time she finally became aware of his erection, hard and, well, *large*, against her hip. Reaching down, she wrapped her fingers around it best she could through his pants, and he groaned, bucking into her hand.

Whatever she'd been intending to say earlier flew out of her mind at the feel of him in her palm. Moving her hand up, she slid it inside his pants and boxer briefs, finally wrapping her fingers fully around him, skin to skin.

He was silky soft and so hard at the same time, and her fingers didn't even meet as she slowly pumped her hand a few times. He groaned again, his eyes tightly closed, and when he opened them, they were kaleidoscope green and yellow, pupils fully elongated.

"Enough of that," he said, his voice gravelly as he pulled out of her grip. "I'm way too close to the edge."

Smiling, she gently pushed him away, sitting up and pulling off her tank top. "Then what are you waiting for?"

He gave a guttural groan as he took her in, and she

hooked her thumbs into her shorts and panties, pulling them off too. He ran his eyes up and down her body, and when he met her eyes again, the heat in his gaze sent a fresh wave of desire through her body.

The way this man could make her feel with just a look was un-freakin'-believable.

He rolled off the bed and pulled his pajama bottoms down and stepped out of them, and her breath caught as she saw all of him. God, he was so gorgeous. Her eyes caught on his reception, long and thick, standing proudly, and her middle clenched.

Holding him in her hand was one thing—seeing him was a whole different ballgame.

He climbed back onto the bed, settling over her, and she let her legs fall open, gasping as his hardness brushed her center. Fire shot straight through her veins, and he leaned down to kiss her as he took himself in hand, rubbing his dick through her folds, coating himself in her wetness.

Every time the head bumped her clit, it sent sparks flying through her, and she gasped as pleasure lit up her nerve endings.

He nipped at her bottom lip—fuck, she loved when he did that—and then pulled back, gazing into her eyes. His were full dragon, so freakin' beautiful, and it turned her on even more. He settled himself at her entrance and then ever so slowly pushed inside.

It'd been a while for her, and she appreciated him going slowly as she felt herself stretching to accommodate him. But the stretch felt amazing, and as much as she probably needed him to go slowly, she didn't want it.

She wanted him buried deeply inside her. Right. Now.

When he was a little more than halfway inside, he paused, leaning down to kiss her passionately. When he pulled pack, he thrust inside her with a powerful push of his hips, and her eyes rolled back in her head. It was a tiny bit painful, but it felt amazing, and pleasure sparked her nerve endings.

He eased out and then thrust forcefully back in, and she moaned as her fingernails dug into his back. That was the rhythm he set, speeding up in increments, until he was rocking forcefully into her. She wrapped her legs around his waist and lifted her hips to meet his thrusts, the sensations he was inspiring inside her nearly overwhelming her.

Rearing back, he put one strong arm under her ass and lifted her up, changing the angle of his thrusts. She moaned as he hit a spot inside her with every thrust that sent pleasure rocketing through her, and then when he set his thumb against her clit and rubbed, that was all it took.

She flew apart, her hips undulating, her vision going black as her breathing stalled. She was drowning in pleasure, and she couldn't draw a breath as it continued washing over her. Her body continued to fly apart, and she could feel herself rippling around Colton, and it just intensified her pleasure and drew it out more.

She was vaguely aware of his hips stuttering, and then he slammed inside her one more time. He held himself still as he emptied himself inside her, and the warmth coating her insides sent her flying up again.

He buried his face in her neck, his body shuddering, as they both came back down. Sucking in air now that she could breath again, she rubbed her hands over his damp back, letting her trembling legs fall to the side.

Her muscles felt weak, and her bones had turned to limp noodles inside her. She didn't think she could move if she tried.

They stayed like they were for what seemed like forever, and she felt her eyes getting heavy. It had been a long time since she'd done anything that physical, and the pleasure she'd drown in had completely depleted her energy.

Colton finally eased back, kissed her gently, and then rolled to the bed next to her. She immediately felt cold, like a piece of her soul had gone missing, and she cuddled up next to him. He wrapped his arm around her, kissing her hair, and she instantly felt warm again.

Her soul felt settled, and her heart was overflowing. This amazing man was holding her tightly, after he'd just given her the most amazing pleasure of her life, and she could barely comprehend how strong her feelings were for him already.

He was sweet, kind, fiercely protective, an amazing lover... everything she never thought she'd find.

And she thought she just might already be in love with him.

Colton was exhausted but his mind was racing, not allowing him to fall asleep just yet. Being with Katia… he never could have imagined he'd feel everything so intensely. He'd heard it was that way between mates, but he still hadn't been expecting *that*.

She was already fast asleep, but he couldn't resist pressing a kiss to her hair. She sighed, snuggling in closer, and a smile curled his lips up.

He was right earlier. He wasn't falling for her—he was already there.

There was still so much up in the air, but he had faith it would all work out. It had to. There was no other option. He'd get Justin back, end the men responsible for hurting him and hunting Katia, and then he could be free to settle down with her.

He loved his small ranch in Montana, but he'd willingly give it up for her. Her life was here, her family, her school. He couldn't ask her to give that up to come to his tiny hometown across the country, but he could damn sure come here to be with her.

He wasn't sure what he'd do with his life once he was here, though. Ranching was all he knew. But he'd figure it out. As long as he had his mate, he'd be okay.

A noise at the door hit his sensitive shifter ears and he stiffened as he turned to look at the door. Easing Katia off his chest, he stood up and silently made his way over, looking out of the peephole. He didn't see anyone there, but that didn't mean there hadn't been.

Even if one of the bastards could hack, that didn't mean they'd be able to find her room, since it wasn't registered in her name. But that didn't necessarily mean anything—they'd set the last hotel on fire, after all.

Looked like he wasn't going to get any sleep tonight after all, because he had to be on alert. If anything happened to her...

Shuddering, he turned to walk back to the bed. He couldn't even begin to imagine what losing her would be like, and he didn't want to. It made him sick to his stomach. She was his—his mate, his life, his everything. He couldn't lose her.

Yeah, it was fast, but that was how it happened for shifters, so it didn't come as much of a surprise to him. She might be a different story. She was human, and they weren't raised with the knowledge that when they met their mate, their entire world shifted and changed, putting their mate at the very center.

That there wasn't anyone else in the world as perfect for them. That no one else could mean as much to them.

He walked over to her side of the bed to switch off the lamp. He wasn't planning on sleeping, but she was, and he could see just as well in the dark as he could in the light, thanks to his shifter sight. Reaching over to switch it off, he bumped into her sketchbook, and it fell to the floor with a soft thud.

Cursing silently, he froze, his gaze shooting to Katia to make sure it didn't wake her. She didn't move, staying relaxed on the bed, her breathing even. Blowing out a breath, he bent to pick up the book, stilling when he saw the page it had fallen open on.

Picking it up, he straightened, studying the drawing. She'd sketched him standing with his arms crossed, a tornado in the background, and on the right was an image of a dragon. It was actually very close to how his dragon really looked, and he felt his eyebrows raise in surprise. The whole drawing was amazing. She'd captured him and his animal very well. It could have been a picture instead of a sketch, it was so accurate.

Curiosity flowed through him and he flipped to the page before, finding an image of his hands, and then another sketch of himself. It was at the hotel they stayed at before, and he was asleep, one arm behind his head and the covers pooling at his waist.

She had so much talent, it was mind blowing.

He looked through the rest of the book, finding images of Sergei and his friends, various people he didn't know, landscapes—she had a little bit of everything in there, and with every picture, he thought they couldn't get better, but they did.

Awe filled him when he was finished, and he closed the book, putting back on the table. Before turning off the light, he looked at her, drinking her in. After the room was doused in darkness, he made his way back around the bed, wondering if there was any way he could help her achieve the dream she truly wanted.

If there was a way to find it, he would.

The moment he settled back onto the bed, she rolled back into him, snuggling close. Heart nearly bursting with warmth and affection, he wrapped her in his arms, contentment and happiness filling his soul.

This amazing woman was his, and he wouldn't let a moment go by when he didn't show or tell her just what she meant to him.

Chapter 8

"Did you always want to work on the ranch?"

Katia asked the question, her eyes roving around the lobby of the hotel. No one else was in there except herself, Colton, and Sergei, who was sitting across the lobby, pretending to read a newspaper. She'd thought Colton would do something similar, but he refused to be far from her, and he was sitting on the floor behind the desk, out of immediate eyesight.

She'd been equal parts exasperated and mushy when he refused to leave her side, but she was glad he had. She enjoyed talking to him and learning more about him. After the night before, she felt incredibly close to him, and every little tidbit she learned just made her feel more so.

"Sort of."

Arching an eyebrow, she slanted a look down at him before returning to watch the lobby. No one had come in for at least forty-five minutes, but she couldn't stop watching. But it wasn't like being hyper vigilant would hurt. It was probably the smart thing to do.

"What does *sort of* mean?"

"Well, I always grew up expecting to be a rancher. But Justin… he wanted to be an Enforcer. It was all he ever talked about, and over time, it became my dream, as well. We tried out and I was accepted but he wasn't—and it crushed him. He talked me into going to training without him, but it didn't feel right without him. And I found it hard to trust people who would turn him down. So, I dropped out and went back to Montana, and did what I originally thought I'd do with my life. Ranching."

She shook her head, her eyebrows raising as she looked at him again. "You gave up your dream for your cousin?"

"It was always his dream, and he wanted it more than I ever did. It eventually became my dream as well, but it was his first. Finishing training and officially becoming an Enforcer just felt all wrong to me, since he wasn't there. And Justin is the best. For them to turn him down because his gift isn't up to their standards… I just couldn't trust them after that. It was a serious lapse in judgment."

Somehow, she thought he *had* wanted it just as much as his cousin. She didn't think he was lying to her about that, but rather lying to himself. He might not have been able to go through with it because Justin wasn't able to, but not doing it hurt him. She could see it lurking in his hazel eyes.

"What exactly is an Enforcer?"

"They're shifter law, basically. They hunt down the evil ones of our kind, the ones who are hurting others, terrorizing humans, or even sometimes the ones who are being too free with the secret. Depending on what the rule breakers have done, they're either sent to shifter prison or put down. The last sounds harsh, but sometimes it's necessary.

"Because of who they hunt, the Enforcers only take the best of the best. You have to be damned near perfect—in top form mentally and physically, able to fight in animal and human form, and you have to have an exceptional gift. Something that can aid in hunting and capturing the bad guys. Justin had it all but the gift. They didn't think his was useful, so they didn't accept him."

She nodded slowly, thinking over what he said. Yeah, putting someone down sounded harsh, especially from a human's perspective, but she could understand it. If there was, say, a dragon who was completely evil, she could understand killing him rather than letting him burn the world down.

She could even understand why they'd want shifters with amazing gifts. They couldn't expect a shifter whose gift was something like speed reading to take on one whose gift was like Colton's. There was no way that could work. But she also thought other qualities could compensate for that. Or putting together a team of Enforcers whose weaknesses were covered by another's strengths.

"So why not do it anyway?" she asked, glancing down.

He looked up at her with an eyebrow cocked. "What, be an Enforcer?"

"Yeah. You and Justin. Go after the bad guys and take them down. Give Justin the training you received before you dropped out, and just do it."

His smile turned rueful. "That would actually be going against shifter laws. If random shifters started trying to do Enforcer missions, it could go south quickly. And then we could end up being the ones hunted by them. We'd be the rogues."

She considered that for a moment and then shrugged. "You'd train Justin, though. And you already said he had it all except the gift. I think yours is good enough to compensate for his. And I really can't see you standing by if someone's in trouble or being hunted by an evil shifter and doing nothing while something bad happened. You'd rush to save them, whether it was against the laws or not. You'd be great at it, and I don't know Justin, but from what you said, he would be too. You could be Rogue Enforcers."

He smiled and she could tell he was trying to pretend that it wasn't a good idea, but she could also see that he was thinking about what she said. She hoped he did, because she thought it was a good idea. Colton was built for a job like that. He had strong protective instincts and his sense of honor was strong, as well. And he already said he was accepted into training and completed most of it, which meant that he had everything else going for him, too.

"Rogue Enforcers. That's a nice play on words there. I'd be a rogue hunting other rogues."

Smiling, she shrugged, scanning the lobby before looking back at him. "But you'd still be the good guy. Promise you'll at least consider it. You'd be amazing at it."

"It wouldn't bother you, being with a law breaker?"

Warmth washed over her. She hadn't thought the night before had been a one-night stand, but his words confirmed that it wasn't. He was talking like they had an indefinite future, and that meant more to her than she could ever express.

"Nope, not at all. You have my complete support if you ever want to do something like that. There are probably a lot of shifters who mostly qualified but were rejected, for whatever reason. It could be bigger than just you and Justin."

He nodded slowly. "I'll think about it."

"You should. Then you could both still have your dream. It might be different than you imagined it to be, but it would be close enough, wouldn't it?"

"It would, especially for Justin. He hasn't been the same since he was rejected. He pretended at first, but it became more and more obvious that he was spiraling." Pausing, his brow furrowed, the look in his eyes saying he was far away in that moment. "At least until a few months ago. He became excited again, with a renewed interest in life. I was happy for him, but he wouldn't tell me what was going on, and then he disappeared."

"Maybe he was doing a little enforcing of his own."

Frown deepening, he looked up at her. "I never considered that, but it makes sense. Why wouldn't he tell me, though?"

She shrugged, watching as someone walked past the front door, relaxing when she realized it wasn't one of the Bad Guys. "Maybe he didn't think you'd approve, or that you'd try to stop him."

He went quiet, his eyes distant as he reached out, putting his big hand on her calf and absentmindedly rubbing his thumb against her bare skin. Breath catching, she squirmed as heat spread over her body.

He wasn't even trying to turn her on, but he was anyway, and it was a little mind blowing that he could do it so easily.

They stayed silent for a while after that, Colton probably thinking about what she said, and Katia still searching for any hint of the creeps. It was him shifting his weight a few times that finally caught her attention, and she glanced down, watching as he did it again.

"Are you okay? You can get up and walk around if you need to."

He huffed a laugh. "I actually need to go to the bathroom, but I don't want to leave you by yourself. I don't suppose you'd consider going with me?"

Shaking her head, she rolled her eyes with a laugh. "Um, no. Just go, Colt. Sergei's still in here, and some of the guys are out front, so I'm not alone. And there's been no sign of them since we got here."

He gazed at her with his eyes narrowed and then finally gave a reluctant nod. "Okay, but don't leave your uncle's sight. I'll be right back."

Her lips curled with amusement as she watched him stand up and walk toward the bathrooms. His protective instincts could be a little overwhelming sometimes, but she couldn't deny that she loved every second of it.

Almost as much as she loved him.

COLTON QUICKLY WASHED HIS HANDS, ANXIOUS TO GET his eyes on Katia again. He hated that he'd had to leave at all, but his bladder had been at the limit, and he had no choice.

He couldn't stop thinking about what she said, though. About starting a group of Rogue Enforcers. It was probably a bad idea, but damn he wanted to, so badly.

Mostly for Justin, but he had to admit it was for himself, too. Not finishing training and becoming a true Enforcer had weighed heavily on him, and even though he'd done his best to put it out of his mind, he just hadn't been able to.

It could be the perfect solution for him, his cousin, and any other shifter who had the skills, but wasn't accepted, for whatever reason.

And the more he thought about it, the more likely

it was that Justin had already been doing some rogue work on his own. It made perfect sense, and he couldn't believe he hadn't thought of it himself.

But he was going to kick his ass for not telling him and putting him through this.

If he hadn't, you might not have met Katia, his dragon pointed out.

That only makes it sort of okay if he's *okay*, he replied as he walked out of the bathroom.

The first thing he saw when he walked in the lobby was Sergei lying still on the floor. David, his friend, was kneeling beside him as he checked his pulse, and Colton put on a burst of speed as his blood ran cold.

Katia wasn't behind the counter. She was gone, and the phone and some other things that had been on the desk were knocked onto the floor, pointing to a struggle. Fear and fury welled up inside him as he sprinted over to where Sergei was lying on the floor.

"What happened? Is he alive?" he barked as he skidded to a stop beside them.

"He has a pulse. I think he'll be all right. Anton and I were in the parking lot when two men came out with Katia. I rushed in here and he followed them. Here, take my cell. Call him. He's following behind them right now. Go get our girl back, and kill the fuckers who did this. Cut off their balls first, though. Make the bastards suffer."

"Damned right, I will."

Taking the cell phone, he rushed to the door, pulling out the keys to his truck as he went. He debated for a moment, and then as soon as he was in his truck, he concentrated for a moment, grim satisfaction filling him as rain poured from the sky, so heavy that it obscured vision.

It was risky. The rain wouldn't fall around his truck, so others could see that it was avoiding him. But it would also slow them down while he could follow faster.

It was a risk he *had* to take.

Rage and worry filled him in equal measure, and he forced himself to blank his thoughts so they didn't overwhelm him. But urgency still rode him hard as he quickly pulled up Anton's number and dialed, putting it on speaker phone before throwing the truck into gear and backing out.

"David?"

"No, this is Colton. He gave me his phone so I could follow you. Where are you?"

"We're about ten miles away, heading out into an area I know well. It's deserted, with no houses or businesses for miles. They were moving fast but this sudden downpour slowed them down."

Fuck. It didn't take a genius to figure out why they were going to a deserted spot. Anton gave him directions and he quickly followed them, cursing as he swerved in and out of traffic. The rain wasn't affecting him, but everyone else had slowed to a crawl, unable to see well enough to drive.

It took longer than he wanted before he could see Anton's car ahead of him. Every second felt like a lifetime while his dragon tore up his chest, just as panicked as he was.

We have to get her back, his dragon hissed. *Let me out when you catch up to them. I'll relish the fear in their eyes before I end them.*

If we're in a deserted enough area, you have my word that you can take them out. Turn into a man eater if you want to. I don't give a shit what you do. Just take those fuckers down.

His dragon hummed with approval, the sound rumbling through the truck. When he was just behind Anton, he spied the black, windowless van in front of him. They were out in the middle of nowhere, with nothing around, and grim pleasure filled him. He could let his dragon out to roast them or eat them—at that point, both sounded like solid options.

He let the rain slowly ease up until there was nothing but drizzle, and then he let that stop, wanting it to seem natural.

"Don't follow too closely," he told Anton. "I don't want them to know we're actually following them. If they turn, don't follow. I'll get out on foot and follow from the main road."

"You got it."

Thankful the other man didn't ask him how he'd be able to easily follow a moving vehicle, he went quiet as they followed behind the van for another three miles. The van slowed and turned onto a dirt road, and he and Anton passed by, slowing to a stop once the trees gave them cover.

Turning off the truck, he quickly got out, meeting Anton by the side of the road. "Thanks for following them. Here's David's phone."

"I'd ask if you need help, but judging by the things your eyes are doing, I don't think you need any," Anton replied in heavily accented English as he studied him. "Even being who I am and doing what I do, I wouldn't mess with you, the way you're looking right now."

"No. I don't. I've got this. Go make sure Sergei's okay."

Anton nodded silently and got back into his car, and he contemplated Anton's words. They made it clear that Sergei and his friends definitely weren't on the right side of the law, but he didn't give a shit about that. Not worrying about concealing his speed or the fact that the other man clearly knew he wasn't quite human, he put on a burst of speed, shooting through the trees.

He caught up with the van just as it was coming to a stop outside of an old, dilapidated barn. Pausing just inside the tree line, he narrowed his eyes, fury filling him when he saw Justin tied up outside of the barn, with a man holding a gun to his head. Justin had a black eye, his clothes were torn and dirty, and he had a bandage wrapped around the hand that was missing a finger.

So, there were at least three of the fuckers, since David said two came in and kidnapped Katia. They'd already die for hurting his cousin, but God help them if they'd harmed a hair on Katia's head. He would break every bone in their bodies and then fry them alive. Maybe even cut off their balls first, like David suggested.

Whatever made them suffer the most.

He normally wasn't a violent man. He'd wanted to be an Enforcer, true, but that was about protecting the innocent, not hurting the accused. He wasn't used to feeling like this, but he welcomed it, feeding off of it, stoking up the desire to end these fuckers for what they'd done.

The man with the gun called out, and another joined him just as the door to the van opened and the men drug a struggling Katia out. His dragon hissed inside him and his fury burned hotter, boiling in his blood, as they dragged her over to the others.

No more men came out. So, there were four. That was child's play for a dragon. He just had to make sure he could take them out before they hurt his mate or Justin.

One of them shoved Katia roughly toward Justin, and she stumbled, just barely catching herself when she started to fall. Turning, her eyes so furious he could see it even from the distance between them, she spit at the man who shoved her.

Pride filled him that she wasn't cowering in terror and instead was fighting back in any way she could. The other man who kidnapped her had scratches down his cheek that were bleeding, showing that she hadn't gone easily, and he was so fucking proud of her for not backing down, even knowing what they could do.

The man raised his hand to hit her, and that was it for him. Katia was glaring, not backing down an inch. He'd hoped for a bit more time to get the lay of the land, but he wasn't going to stand there and do nothing while she was hurt.

"Touch her and die," he growled, walking out of the woods.

In an instant, he had four guns pointed at him, but he didn't stop walking toward them until one of them swung the gun toward Katia. He came to a stop then about twenty feet away, glaring a cold death at the man who had a gun pointed at his mate.

The man swallowed nervously, his eyes betraying the fear he felt, but he stupidly kept his gun pointed at her. He decided that one would definitely die first.

"Who the hell are you?" one of the men demanded.

"That's the one who had the girl. Fucker kept evading us until he stupidly brought her back to her hotel."

"Or maybe not so stupidly," Colton replied, smiling coldly. "Did you not consider that it was a deliberate move?"

The first man who spoke narrowed his eyes, scanning the woods for a moment. "It was fucking idiotic if you thought you could come here and save her alone. Should have stayed out of this. Making it your business means making sure you die."

"You made it my business when you took my

cousin and then my girl," he said with a deceptively casual shrug. "And the only ones dying today are you four for daring to touch either of them."

"Do you see his eyes," one of them said in a low voice. "He's one of them."

"Must be, if that asshole is his cousin. His eyes look different, though. I'm thinking he's not an owl."

"That right?" the first one, clearly the leader, asked. "You a shifter, but not an owl?" Walking over to Justin, he pulled out a knife and placed it against his neck. "Just what kind of animal is your cousin, asshole?"

"I wouldn't know. We're not all that close."

The leader cursed, his fingers tightening on the knife, before he eased it back with a smile. "That's all right. Now we have two shifters, and it doesn't matter what animal he has. I'm sure he'll be more forthcoming than you were on info, since we have his girlfriend. Greg, get the suppressant."

Shit. He had to shift, now, before they injected him with the suppressant that kept him in his human skin. His dragon was all scales and tough, nearly impenetrable hide, so they'd have to be very lucky to inject him once he was shifted.

Justin gave him a slight nod, and he quickly backed up a few paces, not wanting his shift to inadvertently hurt Katia. Hunching over, he gave his dragon his body, along with his blessing to tear these motherfuckers apart.

Pain exploded through his body as he pushed the shift, loud pops ringing out as his bones broke and reformed. There was a rush and a sense of special distortion as he grew much larger than his human form. Once the change was complete, he threw his head back and roared, past the point of caring whether other humans saw or heard him.

The men stumbled back, horror reflected in their eyes, and he relished it—until the one pointing the gun at Katia discharged it as he stumbled.

Katia cried out, falling to her knees, and a red haze coated his vision as he stared at the fucker who shot her.

Hell yes. This one would definitely die first, and he'd take fucking pleasure in ended his worthless existence.

Chapter 9

Katia stared up in awe at the dragon in front of her. Time seemed to stand still for an eternal moment as she stared at Colton. He was much like she'd imagined, only bigger—much bigger. He was even larger than the barn behind her.

His green scales shimmered iridescently in the sun, and his yellow underbelly almost seemed to glow. His eyes were a blazing kaleidoscope of bright green and yellow, and so beautiful. He had two large, curved horns at the top of his head, and spikes that began at the back of his head, getting larger as they followed his spine all the way down to the tip of his tail.

His freakin' talons were as big as her forearms and lethally sharp, and when he threw his head back and roared, his razor-sharp teeth glinted in the sun.

She'd hate to be the one on the wrong side of his dragon. And judging by the fury in his eyes, these men were drawing their last breaths.

A moment later, time snapped back into motion as a gunshot rang out. Fire seared into her side, and she cried out at the pain, falling to her knees. Shit, that hurt like a motherfucker!

Colton roared again, letting out fire of his own, and she inhaled deeply, wincing at the resulting pain in her side at the motion. Gritting her teeth, she dug deep for strength to block out the pain and moved over to Justin.

One of the men had dropped his knife and she grabbed it, awkwardly sawing through the ropes holding his hands together. There was screaming and roaring going on, and gun shots ringing out, but she kept her focus on her task. She wanted him to get free so he could help Colton.

Colton was a dragon, and she knew there might not be much the humans could do to him, but that didn't mean she wasn't terrified that they'd manage to hurt him—or worse. Justin could at least shift and help.

She finally got him free, but instead of shifting, he gently took her hand and led her into the barn. There was a pile of clothes and other essentials inside, like they'd been settling in for a long stay, and he grabbed one of the shirts and pressed it to her side just as another gunshot rang out.

"What are you doing? Stop that and shift! Go help Colt. I can take care of myself."

"I can't shift right now. Besides, Colt doesn't need my help, and he'd kill me if I left you here like this."

Shaking her head, she leaned against the car behind her—the Camry Justin had been driving before. She felt inexplicably weak, but maybe it was just the pain affecting her. "I'm fine. It's just a flesh wound. Go help Colt."

"I told you, I can't. They injected me with a suppressant that means I can't shift." He glanced down, and when he met her gaze again, his blue eyes were worried. "And that's more than a flesh wound. Even if I *could* shift, I wouldn't leave you alone."

Brow twitching, she glanced down, instantly feeling faint. Her blouse and skirt were soaked with blood, and it was quickly seeping through the shirt Justin had pressed to her wound.

"Holy shit," she replied, knowing her eyes were wide when she glanced up. "That's probably more than just a scratch."

His lips twitched, but the worry never left his dark blue eyes. "It definitely is."

She glanced down again, feeling weak. She wasn't sure if it was because of the sight of all the blood or from the loss of it, but she was grateful when he spoke again. It was clear he was trying to distract her, and she could have kissed him for it.

And she would have—before she met Colton, anyway.

"So, what's your name? I'm assuming you know mine, since my cousin called you his girl."

"Katia. It's nice to meet you, although I wish the circumstances were a bit different."

"Yeah. Sorry about that," he said with a half-smile that didn't come anywhere close to reaching his eyes. "Katia, huh? You're Russian?"

"Yep. From a long line of Russian mafia, apparently."

She'd just been making a stupid joke to distract herself from the pain, but hell, thinking that her family was the mob was more normal than what was going on at this very moment.

"Mafia, huh? Nice. So... you're Colton's mate?"

Her brow furrowed thoughtfully. "I mean, he hasn't called it that, but we're together, if that's what you mean."

"I saw the way he looked at you. That, combined with you being together, means you most likely are."

"I wonder why he didn't tell me."

Justin replied, but her mind was far away as her thoughts started getting hazy. Shit. She'd been injured much worse than she thought. At least it didn't hurt as much as it had, but she didn't think that was a good thing either, since her body was starting to feel a little numb.

The fighting outside stopped, and it was the sudden silence that got her attention and brought her back to the present again. Her mind still felt foggy, but she fought to focus, needing to know Colton was okay.

The fight really hadn't lasted long, but then, he was a dragon. She hadn't expected it to.

He strode into the barn, naked as the day he was born, and she ran her eyes over him, looking for any injuries. He had a wicked looking cut on his arm that was bloody, but other than that, he was fine. And maybe it was her imagination, but it seemed to be healing right before her eyes.

No, wait. He'd told her shifters heal fast. She'd known that, but somehow, it had gotten lost in the foggy recesses of her mind.

Her eyes grew heavy, and with it came the knowledge that she might not have long on this earth. It was a fucking shame, and it felt like it was just her luck.

She'd finally met the man of her dreams, but now she was dying. Life was so damned unfair.

"Fuck," Colton cursed as he fell to his knees beside her. "Katia? Sweetheart. Please. Open your eyes, beautiful."

She hadn't even realized she'd closed them. Forcing them open, she gazed up at him, putting everything she felt for him in her eyes. "I didn't want it to happen like this," she whispered, not even having the strength to speak normally. "I wanted a lifetime with you. But I have to tell you something."

She paused, winded, and he touched her cheek gently, his eyes tortured. "Don't try to talk, love. We'll fix you."

"This is important, though. I love you, Colton. So much. More than I ever thought I could love anyone."

. . .

COLTON

Colton stared at Katia, lying against the car, her life's blood seeping out onto the floor, and he wanted to yell and rage and throw shit. He wanted to destroy the fucking world in that moment, because if he lost her, *his* world would be destroyed.

But he kept all of that out of his gaze, not wanting her to see it, and when she whispered that she loved him, his soul felt like it healed just a little bit, and determination settled over him. He would *not* let her fucking die.

Never.

"I love you too, sweetheart. But you're not dying. Not if I have anything to say about it. How do you feel about becoming an owl shifter?"

He saw Justin stiffen with surprise, but he ignored him, all his attention focused on his mate. His dragon was tearing up his chest, urging him to order Justin to turn her now. But as long as she was conscious to give her approval, he was going to hold out.

"An owl shifter?" she whispered, her eyes wide and hazy.

"Yes. I'd change you myself, but dragons can't turn humans. Justin can, though. Come on, Katia. Say yes. Spend forever with me. Hell, even if you don't want that, just let him turn you so you can live. Even if it's not with me. I just need you to *live*."

"Yes," she whispered, her eyes starting to slide closed before she forced them back open. "I want to spend forever with you."

He smiled at her, relief nearly knocking him over,

and then he looked over at his cousin. "You heard her. Turn my mate."

To Justin's credit, he didn't hesitate. He lifted his uninjured hand and then paused. "You should claim her first before I do this. I don't want to give my owl any ideas."

Fuck, he hadn't even thought of that. He started to ask Katia if that was okay, but her eyes were closed, her breathing choppy and shallow, and he didn't think she'd be able to answer him. Hell, she'd already said she wanted to spend her life with him, so why the fuck was he hesitating?

Panic rushed through him and Colton focused his energy on bringing his talons out. Pushing her blouse off her shoulder, he immediately slashed through her skin, going deep enough to claim her thoroughly as his dragon roared with approval inside him.

The moment he was done, Justin was already there, his owl's talons out, and he made the mark just under Colton's, taking care to go deep enough for it to take.

Holding his breath, praying he wasn't too late, he stared at her, willing her breathing to even out. Taking her hand, he held it tightly, panic, fear, and worry eating him up as his dragon tore his chest up. Agony was ripping through him at the thought that they were too late.

He couldn't fucking live without her. He had no doubts about that.

After what felt like an eternity, her breathing started so calm, becoming deeper and more normal.

Relief washed over him, nearly knocking him over, and he closed his eyes against the onslaught. Sending a prayer heavenward, he pressed a kiss to her knuckles, feeling an unaccustomed sting of emotion against his eyelids.

The last time he cried was when he was five and just lost his parents. But if his eyes were open right now, he knew there'd be tears rolling down his cheeks. That was how intensely he was feeling his emotions, how much he fucking loved her, how much relief he felt that he wasn't losing her, after all.

After he managed to get ahold of himself, he opened his eyes and blew out a breath. Her eyes were still closed, but her color was better, and when he moved the shirt out of the way, her bullet wound was nearly healed. The bullet had been pushed out, and it fell out of the shirt when he moved it.

He stared at it, hating that piece of lead with every fiber of his being. He should have tortured the fucker who shot her, but there hadn't been time. He'd had to take care of all of them before they came in here and tried to finish her off and kill Justin.

"Thank you," he said to his cousin, his voice low and hoarse with emotion.

"Anything for you. And I would have done it regardless if it was needed, but this was my fault. It wouldn't have happened if I hadn't gotten myself into this mess."

"We'll talk about that later. Just know you have my eternal gratitude for saving my mate."

"It's not needed, but you're welcome. Is your truck nearby? I know you keep a spare set of clothes in there. I'll go grab them."

He nodded, never taking his eyes off his mate. "Yeah. It's parked on the main road, by the dirt road leading to this place."

"Okay. I'll be right back."

Justin left, and he ran his gaze over Katia, making sure all was well and her new owl was taking the way it should. He pressed another kiss to her fingers, and they tightened in response. His eyes shot up just as hers started blinking, her long lashes casting shadows on her cheek.

She finally got them open and stared up at him with breathtaking silvery sky-blue eyes, her new animal shining through. Smiling up at him, she brought their joined hands to her lips and pressed a kiss to his knuckles, just as he'd done to hers.

"Hi," she whispered huskily.

"Hey there, gorgeous."

Licking her lips, she cautiously sat up, waving him off when he tried to help. "So, it must have taken then, right? I mean, I'm alive, and I feel good. I'm a shifter now? Man, it feels weird to say that."

Chuckling, he leaned in to kiss her softly, unable to resist. "Yeah. You're a snowy owl, to be exact."

Her eyes widened as her hand went to her chest. "Holy shit."

"What?" he asked anxiously, searching for a wound he might not have seen.

"I—well, I think she just talked to me. A snowy owl. I'm a shifter. I don't even have words for this."

Relief flowed over him that she was okay but worry still niggled at the back of his mind. "Are you very upset?"

Her eyebrows shot up as she looked at him. "About what?"

"That you're a shifter now. That you were shot and dying, and the only way to live was to be turned."

Her gorgeous silvery light blue eyes softened, and she put her hand on his cheek as she shook her head. "No. I would have done absolutely anything to stay in this life with you. To have forever with you. Besides, this means I can actually keep up with you now."

"You already were," he replied softly. "I love you, Katia. So much. The thought of losing you nearly crippled me."

"I love you too. And I understand that. The thought of leaving you did the same to me."

Leaning in, he kissed her gently, slowly deepening it as passion exploded between them. He had no idea how long they kissed, lost to everything but her, until Justin cleared his throat behind him.

"I've got your clothes. You can get dressed any time now. Staring at your naked ass is disturbing."

Chuckling, Colton eased away from her, darting in to nip her lip one more time before he stood to get dressed.

This wasn't quite the ending to the story that he'd imagined. He hated that she'd been hurt, that they had to turn her to save her life. But, as he caught a glimpse of her staring at him hungrily as he dressed, he decided that it worked out perfectly.

He had his mate, the love of his life, his everything, forever now. And there was no way that could be considered anything but perfect.

Chapter 10

"I really am so fucking sorry."

Katia smiled at Justin, shaking her head. This was about the hundredth time he'd apologized to her, and he'd done the same to Colton even more. She appreciated it, but it wasn't needed.

"It's okay. It all worked out in the end, and you gave me an incredible gift by giving me my owl. It's all good."

"The hell it is," Colton muttered as they walked into her room at the hotel. "What the hell were you thinking? What did you get yourself into?"

She perched on the bed, curious to know the answer. After Colton got dressed, her new owl—jeez, would that ever not be weird to say? —had begun scratching at her chest, demanding to be let out.

Colton had said that was normal and walked her through the process of shifting, ordering his cousin out so she could undress and try to shift.

The process of shifting had hurt like a motherfucker but being in owl form had been amazing. It'd taken some adjustment to get used to the body, but she managed it, even flying a tiny bit. Not for long, and she didn't go very high, but it'd been amazing, and such a rush.

After that, they'd piled in Colton's truck and made the trip back to the hotel, the silence only broken by Justin's incessant apologies.

Justin exhaled wearily, rubbing his hand over his light brown hair. "I tried to play Enforcer. I learned there was a group of humans who found out about the existence of shifters. They're finding them, suppressing their animals, and selling them on the black market. I thought I could stop it by myself, which was stupid, I know. I allowed myself to get caught, thinking they'd take me to the leader and the other shifters, and I could end it and set them free. Instead, they kept me, trying to get me to give them locations of other shifters, and I stopped nothing. I didn't even meet the man behind it."

"You're right, that *was* stupid."

She shot a look at Colton and he just shrugged unrepentantly. She knew he'd let go of most of his anger at his cousin, but his annoyance was still clearly visible.

"I saw your truck here the other night and I knew

you were close," Justin continued. "I knew I was in over my head at that point. I hoped you were tracking me, but I wasn't sure if you knew for sure I was there. I goaded them into doing something stupid, so you'd hopefully know I was close, and that's when they did this."

He held up his still bandaged hand and Colton's mouth tightened. She'd asked Justin why he was still wearing it, since she knew as a shifter, the injury itself had probably already healed. He'd gotten a self-conscious look on his face, and she'd realized he was embarrassed by his missing finger.

And now to learn he'd done it on purpose to let Colton know he'd been there and to possibly help find him? That could have backfired big time if Colton hadn't demanded she let him in the room.

And by the thunderous look Colton was giving him, he agreed with her. "That was also a dumbass move, Justin. If I hadn't been sure you were here, I might not have asked Katia to let me in, and I never would have seen it."

"You did, though." Justin went quiet and then exhaled heavily. "I just wish it hadn't been for nothing. I didn't stop shit or free the shifters they haven't sold yet."

"For now, anyway," she muttered.

Colton smirked at her as he shook his head. "You're not gonna stop going there, are you?"

"Nope."

Justin's confused gaze bounced between them. "What are y'all talking about?"

She shrugged. "I think you would have succeeded if you hadn't been working alone."

"She thinks we should start our own Enforcer group. Rogue Enforcers," Colton explained with a half-smile. "For shifters who want to be Enforcers, but just don't have exactly what the true Enforcers demand to become one."

Justin perked up as he looked over at her. "Really?"

Shrugging, she nodded. "It makes sense. From what Colt's said, you had everything but the gift. If you form a team, or even a loose group, whose weaknesses are offset by other's strengths, it could work. Colt's gone through training, and he could do that with anyone who wants to join and give them the skills they need to be effective."

"I think that's an awesome idea."

Colton smiled as he looked over at him. "You would. But really think about this, Justin. It's against shifter law. We could become the ones the true Enforcers hunt. Rogues who are hunting rogues. Besides, how would I even be able to find shifters who've been rejected and want to join?"

"I think if we stay off the radar and don't go after the ones the true Enforcers are going after, it could work. And the answer to finding them is obvious. Skylar. He can sniff out anything about anyone. He'd easily be able to find them."

I think this is a great idea, her owl said inside her,

causing her to jump. She didn't know when she'd ever get used to that. *No, not great, it's brilliant. It gives our mate and our new family their dream, and gives others the chance to have theirs, too.*

Our mate? she asked cautiously, still not sure what the word meant.

Oh, he absolutely is. No question about that. You need to claim him now that he's claimed you. Do it soon.

Her owl fell quiet and she blinked, trying to refocus on the conversation. She'd come back to the mate thing later, when she and Colton were alone.

"Who's Skylar?"

"Someone we grew up with. He's a chicken shifter, and he's the best snoop I've ever met."

Justin nodded. "Yep, with the best cock jokes ever. And he's always wanted to be an Enforcer, too, but they wouldn't accept his animal. He'd totally be down for this."

"Wait," she said, holding up a hand. "There are chicken shifters with mad cock jokes running around?"

Colton laughed. "Yeah. He and his family are the only ones I've known, but I'm sure there must be more. He's always making inappropriate cock jokes. Since, you know, he's a rooster."

Pursing her lips, she nodded, deciding she was going to try not to be surprised by anything else in the new world she was apart of again. "He sounds like an interesting character."

"He is," Justin replied in agreement before looking at Colton. "Go get him and enlist his help. He hangs out with the Blood and Bone Enforcers. You can say hi to Blake and Liam while you're there."

Colton glanced over at her. "They're Enforcers I was in training with." He went quiet for a moment, frowning thoughtfully. "Okay. We'll do this. But we have to be cautious. I'm not trying to be the one hunted and put in shifter prison."

Justin let out a whoop, going over to his cousin and thumping him on the back. "That's what I'm talking about."

"All right now get out of here," Colton ordered with a smirk. "I need some time with my mate."

He glanced over at her. "Thank you for coming up with that idea. And I really am so—"

"Don't say it again," she said with a laugh. "It's all good."

He nodded at her with a warm smile. "Welcome to the family."

Turning, he left the room, presumably going to the one they'd gotten him earlier. Colton stood up and came to the bed, sitting sideways next to her, and she turned to face him.

Brushing her hair behind her ear, he searched her eyes for a moment. "Are you really okay? How are you doing?"

"I promise I'm fine. I've never been better, actually. You don't have to keep asking. I'd tell you if something was wrong, but it's all perfect."

And it really was. Her uncle was completely fine—

he had a lump on his head and he was pissed the hell off, at both being knocked out and her being kidnapped. But he was healthy, with no lasting injuries.

She had the most amazing man she'd ever met sitting next to her, and he loved her. Enough to ask his cousin to turn her when she was dying, so he'd have forever with her.

There was a snowy owl living in her chest, which was still mind blowing to her, but the coolest thing ever. Her senses were enhanced, she felt stronger and just better, all around. And even though she and her animal had just met, it was like they were already in accord. Like they were already friends.

She always felt as if she had a hole in her chest for years, a void she hadn't even realized was there, until her owl was filling it.

And Colton had his cousin back, and his dream was finally in reach again.

Life wasn't just good. It was damned near perfect in that moment.

"What's a mate? You've called me yours, and my owl said the same of you."

His eyes warmed as he took her hand, threading their fingers together. "She did? I love that she's said it already. She's beautiful, by the way. Both of you are, human and animal form alike. You're gorgeous."

Smiling, she tightened her hand around his. "You've already said that, but thank you. I think the same of you. Well, you're not beautiful, exactly. You're gorgeous and sexy, and your dragon is stunning and fierce. But you still didn't answer the question."

Chuckling, he leaned in to kiss her, nipping her bottom lip in the way she loved before he pulled back. "A mate is very special to a shifter. They're rare, and that makes them all the more precious to us. Our human sides can love as many people as we want, but there's only one true mate for each of us, and it's our animal who tells us who they are when we meet them.

"Once we meet our mate, that's it. We're theirs for life, whether they want us or not. We'd do *anything* for them—lie, cheat, steal, kill, die. Anything to keep them safe and happy. Their happiness and safety are our main priority. They're our world, our life, our everything. That's what you are to me. Everything I just said, I feel it burning deep within my chest for you."

Katia's eyes misted over, and she blinked rapidly, trying to hold the tears back. Everything he just said was beautiful, and she felt it burning in her chest, too.

"I feel that. Everything you just said. I feel it for you. God, I love you. It happened so fast, but I can't imagine my life without you now."

"It's like that for shifters," he said softly. "When we meet our mate, it happens just like that. For some humans, too, but not always. Some are more resistant. I lucked the fuck out when I got you for a mate, Katia. You're more than I ever imagined I'd find, and that you were so open to me, to my world... I'm the luckiest mand in the world. I love you too, sweetheart, more than I could ever express."

Leaning in, she kissed him softly, her heart damned near bursting with love and happiness. She was the lucky one, but she knew if she told him that, he'd argue with her until the end of forever.

Which was exactly what she had with him. Forever.

When she pulled pack, she sighed dreamily, unable to help herself. "What's your ranch like? I imagine it's beautiful. I can't wait to see it. Soon, hopefully."

He looked at her with surprise in his hazel eyes. "You want to go there with me? What about school?"

"I mean, I'm not willing to give up all my hard work over the past few years. But I'm sure there are colleges near you that I can transfer my credits to. Besides, while it's still a goal I want to achieve, my dream has shifted. It's now a life with you, building the Rogues, building our life together. I'm not willing to put that on hold, especially for a goal I can accomplish in Montana."

He stared at her in silence for a drawn-out moment, his eyes flickering with his dragon. She felt her owl respond, and she put her hand on her chest, reveling in the sensation.

"You're one hell of a woman, Katia," he said softly. "Let's stay here long enough to make sure there's a college near me you can transfer your credits to. As soon as we find one, we'll go to Montana. If there's not, we'll stay here. I'm not willing to let you put off your goals for me, even if your dreams have shifted."

She smiled, confident they'd be going home soon.

Yeah, it was weird, but his ranch already felt like home to her, even though she'd never seen it. But maybe that was just because of him. She'd feel at home wherever he was.

Standing up, she moved to straddle him, pushing his cowboy hat off. "Now that that's settled. My owl is on me to claim you now, and I think it's an excellent idea. You had your turn," she said, reaching up to trace a finger over her claiming mark, "and now it's mine."

His eyes instantly turned hot, and she fused her mouth to his as they fell back onto the bed. Her body was on fire for him, her heart was full of love, and she was so happy, she was sure it radiated from her pores.

This moment was the beginning of her future with the kind, protective, sexy, absolutely amazing man currently kissing the breath right out of her.

It was the beginning of their forever—and what a beautiful life they were going to have together.

She could see it already, and it was the most breathtaking thing she'd ever seen.

Epilogue

Colton straddled his motorcycle, waiting on the man he was looking for to leave the gates of the Enforcers Academy—the training facility. Skylar's first recruit for the Rogues was Maxwell Carter, a black falcon shifter. He'd been injured during flight training, and as a result, wasn't allowed to finish Enforcer training and become a true Enforcer.

But Colton thought with some rehabilitation on his injured wing, he'd be perfect for the Rogues. He had everything else going for him. He just needed to say the word, and he'd be one of them. But how Skylar managed to find out about him so soon after he was rejected, Colton had no idea—and he honestly wasn't sure he wanted to. Knowing Skylar, it probably involved something illegal, especially since Maxwell hadn't even had a chance to leave the facility yet.

Looking down at the inside of his forearm, he traced his fingers over the tattoo he'd gotten last week. Katia had drawn an image in black of his dragon's face, complete with blazing green eyes, and added Rogue Enforcers to a ribbon above it.

It was completely badass, and her talent still had the ability to surprise him, although it probably shouldn't. Everything she drew was amazing.

She, Justin, and Skylar had decided it should be the Rogue's logo. He went along with it, but to him, it would always be a representation of how his mate saw him, and he loved it for that. So much that he had it tattooed onto him.

The others wanted all Rogues to get the tat, but he wasn't sure about making it a requirement. It felt a little arrogant, but they had a point with why they wanted to—they'd decided that the Rogues didn't need to be a tight knit group. Just a bunch of shifters, doing their best to keep the world safe, and they could be where they wanted to while they did it, as long as they went through training with him first.

But if they were a loose knit group, even if they did all answer to him—which was still hard to swallow, the fact that he was now the leader of a group like this—then they needed a way to recognize another Rogue when they saw them.

The last thing they needed was Rogues killing Rogues on accident, because they didn't know they were on the same team. Then the true Enforcers would definitely be hunting them and taking them out.

He still wasn't sure he wanted to make them all get a tattoo of his likeness, though.

But they had time to decide how they wanted to do it. So far, the only Rogues were Colton, Justin, and Skylar, although they were hoping to add Maxwell to the mix.

And Katia, of course, but only in an administrative capacity. Maybe someday down the road, he'd train her, but not now, not in her condition.

His heart overflowed when he thought of her and how happy they were. It'd only been three months, but they'd been the happiest three months of his life.

She'd found a college with a short commute that would accept her transfer credits, and within a week of claiming each other, they were in Montana. She went to school, he worked the ranch, and in the middle, they planned out the Rogues.

And somewhere, in between all of that, she became pregnant. It hadn't been planned so it came as a shock to both of them, but it shouldn't have. There wasn't a day that had gone by where their passion for each other hadn't overcome them—sometimes more than once—and they'd never used protection.

It had been one of the happiest surprises of his life, and he knew she felt the same.

Life was fucking perfect. He had his cousin back—the *real* Justin, the man he'd been before being rejected by the Enforcers—he had an amazing, talented, gorgeous mate, and now they had a little owl shifter on the way. The baby couldn't be a dragon, since the gene didn't pass through the males, but he was grateful for that, especially if it was a girl. He wouldn't wish a dragon on anyone, not with the way their life and culture were.

And now he had his dream. It wasn't exactly like he'd envisioned it, but he thought it was right for him —and he thought it would be right for others, too.

The clink of the gates opening drew his attention back to the present, and he looked over as a truck roared through the opening. The man driving was large with mocha skin, and he recognized him from the picture Skylar dug up. It was Maxwell.

Revving his motorcycle, he took off after him, thankful the weather was perfect, and he'd been able to ride it instead of his driving his truck.

Colton was thankful for a lot of things, actually. And he'd never, not for one moment, forget to be grateful for all the blessings that had come his way.

COMING SOON TO THE ROGUE ENFORCERS SERIES

Releasing June 2019
Maxwell
By Livell James

Stay tuned for more books by other amazing authors in this shared world!

Here's the Rogue Enforcers lineup:
May 2019- Grace Brennan
June 2019- Livell James
July 2019- Rennie Rivera
August 2019 - PA Vachon
September 2019 - Theresa Hissong
October 2019 - Darlene Tallman
November 2019 - Tracie Douglas
December 2019 - Amy Brock McNew
January 2020 - Liberty Parker
February 2020 - Desiree Lafawn
March 2020 - Samantha McCoy

To keep up to date on all the news, cover reveals, and releases from the Rogue Enforcers series, join the Facebook group!

www.facebook.com/groups/RogueEnforcersreadergroup

COMING SOON

GHOST
By Grace Brennan

Book five in the Blood & Bone Enforcers MC series

Acknowledgments

I have to give a huge thanks to the ten other amazing authors who wanted to join this new shared world. It means so much to me that all of you wanted to write in my world, and I can't express how much.

I hope all of the authors, and all of you readers, enjoy the Rogues as much as I am!

Connect with Grace Brennan

Grace has been writing all her life, but never imagined she'd ever let anyone read her work. *Her eyes only*, for years and years, even though being a published author had been her dream since she was in fourth grade. Then, she had a story in her head that wouldn't stop taking over her every waking moment, and characters who wouldn't shut up, demanding to have their story told. She decided when she sat down to write that this time, she was going to do it right and go all the way—and thus Starry Night Sky was born.

Publishing it and letting others into her head, heart, and soul, was one of the hardest, and most terrifying, things she's ever done, but it was incredibly worth it. She writes paranormal shifter romances because it's her favorite genre as a reader, but she's begun branching out into contemporary, publishing her first book, Finding Their One, book one in the Three Hearts Trilogy, under the pen name Khloe Thomas.

She's lived all over, but she calls Texas home at the moment. She has an adorable little boy, two dogs, and addictions to Gilmore Girls—watching it every night isn't a bad thing, is it?—coffee, and tattoos.

You can follow and reach her at the links above—she welcomes it!—or email her at gracebrennanauthor1@gmail.com.

Sign up for Grace's newsletter and be the first to learn about new releases and upcoming projects. No spam, just info on her books!
Grace Brennan Newsletter:
http://eepurl.com/dvH545

To stay up to date, you can also follow Grace on Facebook:
Grace Brennan's Shifter Haven (reader group)
https://www.facebook.com/groups/gracebrennanshifterhaven/
Facebook Page
https://www.facebook.com/gracebrennanauthor

Other ways to follow Grace
Instagram: @gracebrennanauthor
BookBub: @GraceBrennan

More Books by Grace Brennan

Mountain Mermaids: Sapphire Lake

Under the Sea

Blood & Bone Enforcers MC

Control

Thief

Iced

Shield

War Cats

Zane

Karis

Jameson

Vynn

Kian

Rocky River Fighters

Heart of a Fighter

Fighting for Keeps

Fight Song

Fighting to Win

Red Moon Shifters

Unexpected Mates

Temporary Mates

Forever Mates

Bear Claw Shifters

Starry Night Sky

One Sunny Day

Misty Autumn Morning

Made in the USA
Columbia, SC
02 November 2023